POPPY Z.
BRITE

HIS MOUTH WILL TASTE OF WORMWOOD AND OTHER STORIES

D1148966

PENGUIN BOOKS

PENGUIN BOOKS

Published by the Penguin Group. Penguin Books Ltd, 27 Wrights Lane, London w8 5tz, England. Penguin Books USA Inc., 375 Hudson Street, New York, New York 10014, USA. Penguin Books Australia Ltd, Ringwood, Victoria, Australia. Penguin Books Canada Ltd, 10 Alcorn Avenue, Toronto, Ontario, Canada m4v 3b2. Penguin Books (NZ) Ltd, 182–190 Wairau Road, Auckland 10, New Zealand · Penguin Books Ltd, Registered Offices: Harmondsworth, Middlesex, England · These stories have been taken from *Swamp Foetus* by Poppy Z. Brite, published by Penguin Books in 1995. This edition published 1995 · Copyright © Poppy Z. Brite, 1994. All rights reserved · The moral right of the author has been asserted · Typeset by Datix International Limited, Bungay, Suffolk. Printed in England by Clays Ltd, St Ives plc · Except in the United States of America, this book is sold subject to the condition that it shall not, by way of trade or otherwise, be lent, re-sold, hired out, or otherwise circulated without the publisher's prior consent in any form of binding or cover other than that in which it is published and without a similar condition including this condition being imposed on the subsequent purchaser · 10 9 8 7 6 5 4 3 2 1

CONTENTS

'To the treasures and the pleasures of the grave,' said my friend Louis, and raised his goblet of absinthe to me in drunken benediction.

'To the funeral lilies,' I replied, 'and to the calm pale bones.' I drank deeply from my own glass. The absinthe cauterized my throat with its flavor, part pepper, part licorice, part rot. It had been one of our greatest finds: more than fifty bottles of the now-outlawed liqueur, sealed up in a New Orleans family tomb. Transporting them was a nuisance, but once we had learned to enjoy the taste of wormwood, our continued drunkenness was ensured for a long, long time. We had taken the skull of the crypt's patriarch, too, and it now resided in a velvet-lined enclave in our museum.

Louis and I, you see, were dreamers of a dark and restless sort. We met in our second year of college and quickly found that we shared one vital trait: both of us were dissatisfied with everything. We drank straight whisky and declared it too weak. We took strange drugs, but the visions they brought us were of emptiness, mindlessness, slow decay. The books we read were dull; the artists who sold their colorful drawings on the street w mere hacks in our eyes; the music we heard was never loud enough, never harsh enough to stir us. We were truly jaded, we told one another. For all the impression the world made upon us, our eyes might have been dead black holes in our heads.

For a time we thought our salvation lay in the sorcery wrought by music. We studied recordings of weird nameless dissonances, attended performances of obscure bands at ill-lit filthy clubs. But music did not save us. For a time we distracted ourselves with carnality. We explored the damp alien territory between the legs of any girl who would have us, sometimes separately, sometimes both of us in bed together with one girl or more. We bound their wrists and ankles with black lace, we lubricated and penetrated their every orifice, we shamed them with their own pleasures. I recall a mauve-haired beauty, Felicia, who was brought to wild sobbing orgasm by the rough tongue of a stray dog we trapped. We watched her from across the room, drug-hazed and unstirred.

When we had exhausted the possibilities of women we sought those of our own sex, craving the androgynous curve of a boy's cheekbone, the molten flood of ejaculation invading our mouths. Eventually we turned to one another, seeking the thresholds of pain and ecstasy no one else had been able to help us attain. Louis asked me to grow my nails long and file them into needle-sharp points. When I raked them down his back, tiny beads of blood welled up in the angry tracks they left. He loved to lie still, pretending to submit to me, as I licked the salty blood away. Afterward he would push me down and attack me with his mouth, his tongue seeming to sear a trail of liquid fire into my skin.

But sex did not save us either. We shut ourselves in our room and saw no one for days on end. At last we withdrew to the seclusion of Louis's ancestral home near Baton Rouge. Both his parents were dead – a suicide pact, Louis hinted, or perhaps a suicide and a murder. Louis, the only child, retained the family home and fortune. Built on the edge of a vast swamp, the plantation house loomed sepulchrally out of the gloom that surrounded it always, even in the middle of a summer afternoon. Oaks of primordial hugeness grew in a canopy over the house, their branches like black arms fraught with Spanish moss. The moss was everywhere, reminding me of brittle gray hair, stirring wraithlike in the dank breeze from the swamp. I had the impression that, left too long unchecked, the moss might begin to grow from the ornate window-frames and fluted columns of the house itself.

The place was deserted save for us. The air was heady with the luminous scent of magnolias and the fetor of swamp gas. At night we sat on the veranda and sipped bottles of wine from the family cellar, gazing through an increasingly alcoholic mist at the will-o'-the-wisps that beckoned far off in the swamp. Obsessively we talked of new thrills and how we might get them. Louis's wit sparkled liveliest when he was bored, and on the night he first mentioned grave robbing, I laughed. I could not imagine that he was serious.

'What would we do with a bunch of dried-up old remains? Grind them to make a voodoo potion? I preferred your idea of increasing our tolerance to various poisons.'

Louis's sharp face snapped toward me. His eyes were painfully sensitive to light, so that even in this gloaming he wore tinted glasses and it was impossible to see his expression. He kept his fair hair clipped very short, so that it stood up in crazy tufts when he raked a nervous hand through it. 'No, Howard. Think of it: our own collection of death. A catalogue of pain, of human frailty – all for us. Set against a backdrop of tranquil loveliness. Think what it would be to walk through such a place, meditating, reflecting upon your own ephemeral essence. Think of making love in a charnel-house! We have only to assemble the parts – they will create a whole into which we may fall.'

(Louis enjoyed speaking in cryptic puns; anagrams and palindromes, too, and any sort of puzzle appealed to him. I wonder whether that was not the root of his determination to look into the fathomless eye of death and master it. Perhaps he saw the mortality of the flesh as a gigantic jigsaw or crossword which, if he fitted all the parts into 4 place, he might solve and thus defeat. Louis would have loved to live forever, though he would never have known what to do with all his time.)

He soon produced his hashish pipe to sweeten the taste of the wine, and we spoke no more of grave robbing that night. But the thought preyed upon me in the languorous weeks to come. The smell of a freshly opened grave, I thought, must in its way be as intoxicating as the perfume of the swamp or a girl's most intimate sweat. Could we truly assemble a collection of the grave's treasures that would be lovely to look upon, that would soothe our fevered souls?

The caresses of Louis's tongue grew languid. Sometimes, instead of nestling with me between the black satin sheets of our bed, he would sleep on a torn blanket in one of the underground rooms. These had originally been built for indeterminate but always intriguing purposes – abolitionist meetings had taken place there, Louis told me, and a weekend of free love, and an earnest but wildly incompetent Black Mass replete with a vestal virgin and phallic candles.

These rooms were where our museum would be set up. At last I came to agree with Louis that only the plundering of graves might cure us of the most stifling ennui we had yet suffered. I could not bear to watch his tormented sleep, the pallor of his hollow cheeks, the delicate bruise-like darkening of the skin beneath his flickering eyes. Besides, the notion of grave robbing had begun to entice 5 me. In ultimate corruption, might we not find the path to ultimate salvation?

Our first grisly prize was the head of Louis's mother, rotten as a pumpkin forgotten on the vine, half-shattered by two bullets from an antique Civil War revolver. We took it from the family crypt by the light of a full moon. The will-o'-the-wisps glowed weakly, like dying beacons on some unattainable shore, as we crept back to the manse. I dragged pick and shovel behind me; Louis carried the putrescent trophy tucked beneath his arm. After we had descended into the museum, I lit three candles scented with the russet spices of autumn (the season when Louis's parents had died) while Louis placed the head in the alcove we had prepared for it. I thought I detected a certain tenderness in his manner. 'May she give us the family blessing,' he murmured, absently wiping on the lapel of his jacket a few shreds of pulpy flesh that had adhered to his fingers.

We spent a happy time refurbishing the museum, polishing the inlaid precious metals of the wall fixtures, brushing away the dust that frosted the velvet designs of the wallpaper, alternately burning incense and charring bits of cloth we had saturated with our blood, in order to give the rooms the odor we desired – charnel perfume strong enough to drive us to frenzy. We travelled far in our collections, but always we returned home with crates full of things no

6   man had ever been meant to possess. We heard of a girl

with violet eyes who had died in some distant town; not seven days later we had those eyes in an ornate cut-glass jar, pickled in formaldehyde. We scraped bone dust and nitre from the bottoms of ancient coffins; we stole the barely withered heads and hands of children fresh in their graves, with their soft little fingers and their lips like flower petals. We had baubles and precious heirlooms, vermiculated prayer-books and shrouds encrusted with mold. I had not taken seriously Louis's talk of making love in a charnel-house – but neither had I reckoned on the pleasure he could inflict with a femur dipped in rose-scented oil.

Upon the night I speak of – the night we drank our toast to the grave and its riches – we had just acquired our finest prize yet. Later in the evening we planned a celebratory debauch at a nightclub in the city. We had returned from our most recent travels not with the usual assortment of sacks and crates, but with only one small box carefully wrapped and tucked into Louis's breast pocket. The box contained an object whose existence we had only speculated upon previously. From certain half-articulate mutterings of an old blind man plied with cheap liquor in a French Quarter bar, we traced rumors of a certain fetish or charm to a Negro graveyard in the southern bayou country. The fetish was said to be a thing of eerie beauty, capable of luring any lover to one's bed, hexing any enemy to a sick and painful death, and (this, I think, was   7 what intrigued Louis the most) turning back tenfold on anyone who used it with less than the touch of a master.

A heavy mist hung low over the graveyard when we arrived there, lapping at our ankles, pooling around the markers of wood and stone, abruptly melting away in patches to reveal a gnarled root or a patch of blackened grass, then closing back in. By the light of a waning moon we made our way along a path overgrown with rioting weeds. The graves were decorated with elaborate mosaics of broken glass, coins, bottlecaps, oyster shells lacquered silver and gold. Some mounds were outlined by empty bottles shoved neck-downward into the earth. I saw a lone plaster saint whose features had been worn away by years of wind and rain. I kicked half-buried rusty cans that had once held flowers; now they held only bare brittle stems and pestilent rainwater, or nothing at all. Only the scent of wild spider lilies pervaded the night.

The earth in one corner of the graveyard seemed blacker than the rest. The grave we sought was marked only by a crude cross of charred and twisted wood. We were skilled at the art of violating the dead; soon we had the coffin uncovered. The boards were warped by years of burial in wet, foul earth. Louis pried up the lid with his spade and, by the moon's meager and watery light, we gazed upon what lay within.

Of the inhabitant we knew almost nothing. Some said a
8 hideously disfigured old conjure woman lay buried here.

Some said she was a young girl with a face as lovely and cold as moonlight on water, and a soul crueler than Fate itself. Some claimed the body was not a woman's at all, but that of a white voodoo priest who had ruled the bayou. He had features of a cool, unearthly beauty, they said, and a stock of fetishes and potions which he would hand out with the kindest blessing . . . or the direst curse. This was the story Louis and I liked best; the sorcerer's capriciousness appealed to us, and the fact that he was beautiful.

No trace of beauty remained to the thing in the coffin — at least not the sort of beauty that a healthy eye might cherish. Louis and I loved the translucent parchment skin stretched tight over long bones that seemed to have been carved from ivory. The delicate brittle hands folded across the sunken chest, the soft black caverns of the eyes, the colorless strands of hair that still clung to the fine white dome of the skull — to us these things were the poetry of death.

Louis played his flashlight over the withered cords of the neck. There, on a silver chain gone black with age, was the object we had come seeking. No crude wax doll or bit of dried root was this. Louis and I gazed at each other, moved by the beauty of the thing; then, as if in a dream, he reached to grasp it. This was our rightful night's prize, our plunder from a sorcerer's grave.

'How does it look?' Louis asked as we were dressing.

I never had to think about my clothes. On an evening such as this, when we were dressing to go out, I would choose the same garments I might wear for a night's digging in the graveyard – black, unornamented black, with only the whiteness of my face and hands showing against the backdrop of night. On a particularly festive occasion, such as this, I might smudge a bit of kohl round my eyes. The absence of color made me nearly invisible: if I walked with my shoulders hunched and my chin tucked down, no one except Louis would see me.

'Don't slouch so, Howard,' said Louis irritably as I ducked past the mirror. 'Turn around and look at me. Aren't I fine in my sorcerer's jewelry?'

Even when Louis wore black, he did it to be noticed. Tonight he was resplendent in narrow-legged trousers of purple paisley silk and a silvery jacket that seemed to turn all light iridescent. He had taken our prize out of its box and fastened it around his throat. As I came closer to look at it, I caught Louis's scent: rich and rather meaty, like blood kept too long in a stoppered bottle.

Against the sculpted hollow of Louis's throat, the thing on its chain seemed more strangely beautiful than ever. Have I neglected to describe the magical object, the voodoo fetish from the churned earth of the grave? I will never forget it. A polished sliver of bone (or a tooth, but what fang could have been so long, so sleekly honed, and still have somehow retained the look of a *human tooth*?) bound by a strip of copper. Set into the metal, a single ruby sparkled like a drop of gore against the verdigris. Etched in exquisite miniature upon the sliver of bone, and darkened by the rubbing in of some black-red substance, was an elaborate veve – one of the symbols used by voodooists to invoke their pantheon of terrible gods. Whoever was buried in that lonely bayou grave, he had been no mere dabbler in swamp magic. Every cross and swirl of the veve was reproduced to perfection. I thought the thing still retained a trace of the grave's scent – a dark odor like potatoes long spoiled. Each grave has its own peculiar scent, just as each living body does.

'Are you certain you should wear it?' I asked.

'It will go into the museum tomorrow,' he said, 'with a scarlet candle burning eternally before it. Tonight its powers are mine.'

The nightclub was in a part of the city that looked as if it had been gutted from the inside out by a righteous tongue of fire. The street was lit only by occasional scribbles of neon high overhead, advertisements for cheap hotels and all-night bars. Dark eyes stared at us from the crevices and pathways between buildings, disappearing only when Louis's hand crept toward the inner pocket of his jacket. He carried a small stiletto there, and knew how to use it for more than pleasure.

We slipped through a door at the end of an alley and descended the narrow staircase into the club. The lurid glow of a blue bulb flooded the stairs, making Louis's face look sunken and dead behind his tinted glasses. Feedback blasted us as we came in, and above it, a screaming battle of guitars. The inside of the club was a patchwork of flickering light and darkness. Graffiti covered the walls and the ceiling like a tangle of barbed wire come alive. I saw bands' insignia and jeering death's-heads, crucifixes bejewelled with broken glass and black obscenities writhing in the stroboscopic light.

Louis brought me a drink from the bar. I sipped it slowly, still drunk on absinthe. Since the music was too loud for conversation, I studied the clubgoers around us. A quiet bunch, they were, staring fixedly at the stage as if they had been drugged (and no doubt many of them had – I remembered visiting a club one night on a dose of hallucinogenic mushrooms, watching in fascination as the guitar strings seemed to drip soft viscera onto the stage). Younger than Louis and myself, most of them were, and queerly beautiful in their thrift shop rags, their leather and fishnet and cheap costume jewelry, their pale faces and painted hair. Perhaps we would take one of them home with us tonight. We had done so before. 'The delicious guttersnipes,' Louis called them. A particularly beautiful face, starkly boned and androgynous, flickered at the edge of my vision. When I looked, it was gone.

I went into the restroom. A pair of boys stood at a single urinal, talking animatedly. I stood at the sink rinsing my hands, watching the boys in the mirror and trying to overhear their conversation. A hairline fracture in the glass seemed to pull the taller boy's eyes askew. 'Caspar and Alyssa found her tonight,' he said. 'In some old warehouse by the river. I heard her skin was *gray*, man. And sort of withered, like something had sucked out most of the meat.'

'Far out,' said the other boy. His black-rimmed lips barely moved.

'She was only fifteen, you know?' said the tall boy as he zipped his ragged trousers.

'She was a cunt anyway.'

They turned away from the urinal and started talking about the band – Ritual Sacrifice, I gathered, whose name was scrawled on the walls of the club. As they went out, the boys glanced at the mirror and the tall one's eyes met mine for an instant. Nose like a haughty Indian chief's, eyelids smudged with black and silver. Louis would approve, I thought – but the night was young, and there were many drinks left to be had.

When the band took a break we visited the bar again. Louis edged in beside a thin dark-haired boy who was barechested except for a piece of torn lace tied about his throat. When he turned, I knew his was the androgynous and striking face I had glimpsed before. His beauty was almost feral, but overlaid with a cool elegance like a veneer of sanity hiding madness. His ivory skin stretched over cheekbones like razors; his eyes were hectic pools of darkness.

'I like your amulet,' he said to Louis. 'It's very unusual.'

'I have another one like it at home,' Louis told him.

'Really? I'd like to see them both together.' The boy paused to let Louis order our vodka gimlets, then said, 'I thought there was only one.'

Louis's back straightened like a string of beads being pulled taut. Behind his glasses, I knew, his pupils would have shrunk to pinpoints: the light pained him more when he was nervous. But no tremor in his voice betrayed him when he said, 'What do you know about it?'

The boy shrugged. On his bony shoulders, the movement was insouciant and drop-dead graceful. 'It's voodoo,' he said. 'I know what voodoo is. Do you?'

The implication stung, but Louis only bared his teeth the slightest bit; it might have been a smile. 'I am *conversant* in all types of magic,' he said, 'at least.'

The boy moved closer to Louis, so that their hips were almost touching, and lifted the amulet between thumb and forefinger. I thought I saw one long nail brush Louis's throat, but I could not be sure. 'I could tell you the meaning of this veve,' he said, 'if you were certain you wished to know.'

'It symbolizes power,' Louis said. 'All the power of my soul.' His voice was cold, but I saw his tongue dart out to moisten his lips. He was beginning to dislike this boy, and also to desire him.

'No,' said the boy so softly that I barely caught his words. He sounded almost sad. 'This cross in the center is inverted, you see, and the line encircling it represents a serpent. A thing like this can trap your soul. Instead of being rewarded with eternal life . . . you might be doomed to it.'

'Doomed to eternal life?' Louis permitted himself a small cold smile. 'Whatever do you mean?'

'The band is starting again. Find me after the show and I'll tell you. We can have a drink . . . and you can tell me all you know about voodoo.' The boy threw back his head and laughed. Only then did I notice that one of his upper canine teeth was missing.

The next part of the evening remains a blur of moonlight and neon, ice cubes and blue swirling smoke and sweet drunkenness. The boy drank glass after glass of absinthe with us, seeming to relish the bitter taste. None of our other guests had liked the liqueur. 'Where did you get it?' he asked. Louis was silent for a long moment before he said, 'It was sent over from France.' Except for its single black gap, the boy's smile would have been as perfect as the sharp-edged crescent moon.

15

'Another drink?' said Louis, refilling both our glasses.

When I next came to clarity, I was in the boy's arms. I could not make out the words he was whispering; they might have been an incantation, if magic may be sung to pleasure's music. A pair of hands cupped my face, guiding my lips over the boy's pale parchment skin. They might have been Louis's hands. I knew nothing except this boy, the fragile movement of the bones beneath the skin, the taste of his spit bitter with wormwood.

I do not remember when he finally turned away from me and began lavishing his love upon Louis. I wish I could have watched, could have seen the lust bleeding into Louis's eyes, the pleasure racking his body. For, as it turned out, the boy loved Louis so much more thoroughly than ever he loved me.

When I awoke, the bass thump of my pulse echoing through my skull blotted out all other sensations. Gradually, though, I became aware of tangled silk sheets, of hot sunlight on my face. Not until I came fully awake did I see the thing I had cradled like a lover all through the night.

For an instant two realities shifted in uneasy juxtaposition and almost merged. I was in Louis's bed; I recognized the feel of the sheets, their odor of silk and sweat. But this thing I held – this was surely one of the fragile mummies we had dragged out of their graves, the things we dissected for our museum. It took me only a moment, though, to recognize the familiar ruined features – the sharp chin, the high elegant brow. Something had desiccated Louis, had drained him of every drop of his moisture, his vitality. His skin crackled and flaked away beneath my fingers. His hair stuck to my lips, dry and colorless. The amulet, which had still been around his throat in bed last night, was gone.

The boy had left no trace – or so I thought until I saw a nearly transparent thing at the foot of the bed. It was like a quantity of spiderweb, or a damp and insubstantial veil. I picked it up and shook it out, but could not see its features until I held it up to the window. The thing was vaguely human-shaped, with empty limbs trailing off into nearly invisible tatters. As the thing wafted and billowed, I saw part of a face in it – the sharp curve left by a cheekbone, the hole where an eye had been – as if a face were imprinted upon gauze.

I carried Louis's brittle shell of a corpse down into the museum. Laying him before his mother's niche, I left a stick of incense burning in his folded hands and a pillow of black silk cradling the papery dry bulb of his skull. He would have wished it thus.

The boy has not come to me again, though I leave the window open every night. I have been back to the club, where I stand sipping vodka and watching the crowd. I have seen many beauties, many strange wasted faces, but not the one I seek. I think I know where I will find him. Perhaps he still desires me – I must know.

I will go again to the lonely graveyard in the bayou. Once more – alone, this time – I will find the unmarked grave and plant my spade in its black earth. When I open the coffin – I know it, I am sure of it – I will find not the mouldering thing we beheld before, but the calm beauty of replenished youth. The youth he drank from Louis. His face will be a scrimshaw mask of tranquility. The amulet – I know it; I am sure of it – will be around his neck.

Dying: the final shock of pain or nothingness that is the price we pay for everything. Could it not be the sweetest thrill, the only salvation we can attain . . . the only true moment of self-knowledge? The dark pools of his eyes will open, still and deep enough to drown in. He will hold out his arms to me, inviting me to lie down with him in his rich wormy bed.

With the first kiss his mouth will taste of wormwood. After that it will taste only of me – of my blood, my life, siphoning out of my body and into his. I will feel the sensations Louis felt: the shrivelling of my tissues, the drying-up of all my vital juices. I care not. The treasures and the pleasures of the grave? They are his hands, his lips, his tongue.

The Sixth Sentinel

I first knew hard-luck Rosalie Smith when she was a thin frayed rope of a child, twenty years old and already well acquainted with the solitude at the bottom of a whisky bottle. Her hair was brittle from too many dye jobs, bright red last week, black as the grave today, purple and green for Mardi Gras. Her face was fine-boned and faintly feral, the eyes carefully lined in black, the rouged lips stretched tight over the sharp little teeth. If I had been able to touch Rosalie, her skin would have felt silky and faintly dry, her hair would have been like electricity brushing my face in the dark.

But I could not touch Rosalie, not so that she would notice. I could pass my fingers through the meat of her arm, pale as veal and packed like flaky fish flesh between her thin bones. I could wrap my hand around the smooth porcelain ball of her wrist. But as far as she was concerned, my touch went through her like so much dead air. All she could feel of me was a chill like ice crystallizing along her spine.

'Your liver has the texture of hot, wet velvet,' I would tell her, reaching through her ribs to caress the tortured organ.

She'd shrug. 'Another year in this town and it'll be pickled.'

Rosalie came to the city of New Orleans because it was as far south as her money would take her – or so she said. She was escaping from a lover she would shudderingly refer to only as Joe Coffeespoon. The memory of his touch made her feel cold, far colder than my ectoplasmic fingers ever could, and she longed for the wet kiss of tropical nights.

She moved into an apartment in one of the oldest buildings in the French Quarter, above a 'shoppe' that sold potions and philters. At first I wondered whether she would be pleased to find a ghost already residing in her cramped quarters, but as I watched her decorate the walls with shrouds of black lace and photographs of androgynous sunken-cheeked musicians who looked more dead than alive, I began to realize I could show myself safely, without threat of eviction. It is always a nuisance when someone calls in the exorcist. The priest himself is no threat, but the demons that invariably follow him are large as cats and annoying as mosquitoes. It is these, not the intonations and holy water, that drive innocent spirits away.

But Rosalie only gave me a cool appraising look, introduced herself, then asked me for my name and my tale. The name she recognized, having seen it everywhere from the pages of history books to the shingles hanging outside

dubious 'absinthe' houses in the French Quarter. The tale
– well, there were enough tales to entertain her for a
thousand nights or more. (I, the Scheherazade of Barataria
Bay!) How long had I wanted to tell those tales? I had
been without a friend or a lover for more years than I
could recall. (The company of other local ghosts did not
interest me – they seemed a morbid lot, many of them
headless or drenched in gore, manifesting only occasionally
to point skeletal fingers at loose fireplace flagstones and
then vanish without a word. I had met no personalities of
substance, and certainly none with a history as exotic as
mine.)

So I was glad for the company of Rosalie. As more old
buildings are demolished I must constantly shift about the
city, trying to find places where I resided in life, places
where a shred of my soul remains to anchor me. There are
still overgrown bayou islands and remote Mississippi coves
I visit often, but to give up the drunken carnival of New
Orleans, to forsake human companionship (witting or
otherwise) would be to fully accept my death. Nearly two
hundred years, and I still cannot do that.

'Jean,' she would say to me as evening fell like a slowly
drifting purple scarf over the French Quarter, as the
golden flames of the streetlights flickered on, 'do you like
these panties with the silver bustier, Jean?' (She pro-
nounced my name correctly, in the French manner, like
John but with the soft J.) Five nights of the week Rosalie

had a job stripping at a nightclub on Bourbon Street. She selected her undress from a vast armoire crammed full of the microscopic wisps of clothing she referred to as 'costumes', some of which were only slightly more substantial than my own flesh. When she first told me of the job she thought I would be shocked, but I laughed. 'I saw worse things in my day,' I assured her, thinking of lovely, shameless octoroon girls I had known, of famous 'private shows' involving poisonous serpents sent from Haiti and the oiled stone phalluses of alleged voodoo idols.

I went to see Rosalie dance two or three times. The strip club was in an old row building, the former site of a bordello I remembered well. In my day the place had been decorated entirely in scarlet silk and purple velvet; the effect was of enormous fleshy lips closing in upon you as you entered, drawing you into their dark depths. I quit visiting Rosalie at work when she said it unnerved her to suddenly catch sight of me in the hundreds of mirrors that now lined the club, a hundred spangle-fleshed Rosalies and a hundred translucent Jeans and a thousand pathetic weasel-eyed men all reflected to a point of swarming infinity far within the walls. I could see how the mirrors might make Rosalie nervous, but I believe she did not like me looking at the other dancers either, though she was the prettiest of a big-hipped, insipid-faced lot.

By day Rosalie wore black: lace and fishnet, leather and silk, the gaudy mourning clothes of the deather-children.

I had to ask her to explain them to me, these deathers. They were children seldom older than eighteen who painted their faces stark white, rimmed their eyes with kohl, smudged their mouths black or blood-red. They made love in cemeteries, then plundered the rotting tombs for crucifixes to wear as jewelry. The music they listened to was alternately lush as a wreath of funeral roses and dark as four a.m., composed in suicidal gloom by the androgynes that decorated Rosalie's walls. I might have been able to tell these children a few things about death. Try drifting through a hundred years without a proper body, I might have said, without feet to touch the ground, without a tongue to taste wine or kiss. Then perhaps you will celebrate your life while you have it. But Rosalie would not listen to me when I got on this topic, and she never introduced me to any of her deather friends.

If she had any. I had seen other such children roaming the French Quarter after dark, but never in Rosalie's company. Often as not she would sit in her room and drink whiskey on her nights off, tipping inches of liquid amber fire over crackling ice cubes and polishing it off again, again, again. She never had a lover that I knew of, aside from the dreaded Coffeespoon, who it seemed had been quite wealthy by Rosalie's standards. Her customers at the club offered her ludicrous sums if she would only grant them one night of pleasure more exotic than their toadlike minds could imagine. A few might really have been able to pay such fortunes, but Rosalie ignored their tumescent pleading. She seemed not so much opposed to the idea of sex for money as simply uninterested in sex at all.

When she told me of the propositions she received, I thought of the many things I had buried in the earth during my days upon it. Treasure: hard money and jewels, the riches of the robbery that was my bread and butter, the spoils of the murder that was my wine. There were still caches that no one had found and no one ever would. Any one of them would have been worth ten times the amounts these men offered.

Many times I tried to tell Rosalie where these caches were, but unlike some of her kind, she thought buried things should stay buried. She claimed that the thought of the treasure hidden under mud, stone, or brick, with people walking near it and sometimes right over it each day, amused her more than the thought of digging it up and spending it.

I never believed her. She would not let me see her eyes when she said these things. Her voice trembled when she spoke of the deathers who pursued grave-robbing as a sport. ('They pried up a granite slab that weighed fifty pounds,' she told me once, incredulously. 'How could they bear to lift it off, in the dark, not knowing what might come out at them?') There was a skeleton in a glass-topped coffin downstairs, in the voodoo shoppe, and Rosalie hardly liked to enter the shoppe because of it – I had seen her glancing out of the corner of her eye, as if the sad little bones simultaneously intrigued and appalled her.

It was some obsessive fear of hers, I realized. Rosalie shied away from all talk of dead things, of things buried, of digging in the ground. When I told her my tales she made me skip over the parts where treasures or bodies were buried; she would not let me describe the fetor of the night-time swamp, the faint flickering lights of St Elmo's fire, the deep sucking sound the mud made when a shovel was thrust into it. She would allow me no descriptions of burials at sea or shallow bayou graves. She covered her ears when I told her of a rascal whose corpse I hung from the knotted black bough of a hundred-year-old oak. It was a remarkable thing, too – when I rode past the remote spot a year later, his perfect skeleton still hung there, woven together by strands of gray Spanish moss. It wound around his long bones and cascaded from the empty sockets of his eyes, it forced his jaws open and dangled from his chin like a long gray beard – but Rosalie did not want to hear about it.

When I confronted her with her own dread, she refused to own up to it. 'Whoever said graveyards were romantic?' she demanded. 'Whoever said I had to go digging up bones just because I lust after Venal St Claire?' (Venal St Claire was a musician, one of the stick-thin, mourning- 25 shrouded beauties that adorned the walls of Rosalie's room. I saw no evidence that she lusted after him or anyone else.) 'I just wear black so that all my clothes will match,' she told me solemnly, as if she expected me to believe it. 'So I won't have to think about what to put on when I get up in the morning.'

'But you *don't* get up in the morning.'

'In the evening, then. *You* know what I mean.' She tipped her head back and tongued the last drop of whiskey out of her glass. It was the most erotic thing I had ever seen her do. I ran my finger in among the smooth folds of her intestines. A momentary look of discomfort crossed her face, as if she had suffered a gas pain – attributable to the rotgut whiskey, no doubt. But she would not pursue the subject further.

So I watched her drink until she passed out, her brittle hair fanned across her pillow, the corner of her mouth drooling a tiny thread of spit on to her black silk coverlet. Then I went into her head. This was not a thing I liked to do often – on occasion I had noticed her looking askance at me the morning after, as if she remembered seeing me in her dreams and wondered how I had got there. If I could persuade Rosalie to dig up one cache of loot – just one – our troubles would end. She would never have to work again, and I could have her with me all the time. But first I had to find her fear. Until I knew what it was, and could figure out how to charm my way around it, my treasures were going to stay buried in black bayou mud.

So within moments I was sunk deep in the spongy tissue of Rosalie's brain, sifting through her childhood memories as if they were gold coins I had just lifted off a Spanish galleon. I thought I could smell the whiskey that clouded her dreams, a stinging mist.

I found it more quickly than I expected to. I had reminded Rosalie of her fear, and now – because she would not let her conscious mind remember – her unconscious mind was dreaming of it. For an instant I teetered on the edge of wakefulness; I was dimly aware of the room around me, the heavy furniture and flocked black walls. Then it all swam away as I fell headlong into Rosalie's childhood dream.

A South Louisiana village, built at the confluence of a hundred streams and rivulets. Streets of dirt and crushed oyster-shells, houses built on pilings to keep the water from lapping up onto the neat, brightly painted porches. Shrimp nets draped over railings, stiffening with salt, at some houses; crab traps stacked up to the roof at others. Cajun country.

(Hard-luck Rosalie, a Cajun girl, she who claimed she had never set foot in Louisiana before! *Mon petit chou!* 'Smith' indeed!)

On one porch a young girl dressed in a T-shirt and a home-sewn skirt of fresh calico perches on a case of empty beer bottles. The tender points of her breasts can be seen through the thin fabric of the T-shirt. A medallion gleams at the hollow of her throat, a tiny saint frozen in silver. She is perhaps twelve. It can only be her mama beside her, a large regal-faced woman with a crown of teased and fluffed black hair. The mama is peeling crawfish. She saves the heads in a coffee can and throws the other pickings to some speckled chickens scratching in the part of the dirt yard that is not flooded. The water is as high as Mama has ever seen it. The young girl has a can of Coca-Cola, but she hasn't drunk much of it. She is worried about something: it can be seen in the slump of her shoulders, in the sprawl of her thin legs beneath the calico skirt. Several times her eyes shimmer with tears she is just able to control. When she looks up, it becomes clear that she is older than she appeared at first, thirteen or fourteen. An air of naivete, an awkwardness of limb and gesture, makes her seem younger. She fidgets and at last says, 'Mama?'

'What is it, Rosie?' The mother's voice seems a beat too slow; it catches in her throat and drags itself reluctantly out past her lips.

'Mama – is Theophile still under the ground?'

(There is a gap in the dream here, or rather in my awareness of it. I do not know who Theophile is – a childhood friend perhaps. More likely a brother; in a Cajun family there is no such thing as an only child. The question disturbs me, and I feel Rosalie slipping from me momentarily. Then the dream continues, inexorable, and I am pulled back in.)

Mama struggles to remain calm. Her shoulders bow and her heavy breasts sag against her belly. The stoic expression on her face crumbles a little. 'No, Rosie,' she says at last. 'Theophile's grave is empty. He's gone up to Heaven, him.'

'Then he wouldn't be there if I looked?'

(All at once I am able to recognize my Rosalie in the face of this blossoming girl. The intelligent dark eyes, the quick mind behind them undulled by whisky and time.)

Mama is silent, searching for an answer that will both satisfy and comfort. But a bayou storm has been blowing up, and it arrives suddenly, as they will: thunder rolls across the sky, the air is suddenly alive with invisible sparks. Then the rain comes down in a solid torrent. The speckled chickens scramble under the porch, complaining. Within seconds the yard in front of the house is a sea of mud. It has rained like this every day for a month. It is the wettest spring anyone has ever seen in this part of the bayou.

'You ain't goin' anywhere in this flood,' Mama says. The relief is evident in her voice. She shoos the girl inside and hurries around the house to take washing off the line, though the faded cotton dresses and patched denim trousers are already soaked through.

Inside the warm little house, Rosalie sits at the kitchen window watching rain hammer down on the bayou, and she wonders.

The storm lasts all night. Lying in her bed, Rosalie hears the rain on the roof; she hears branches creaking and lashing in the wind. But she is used to thunderstorms, and she pays no attention to this one. She is thinking of a shed in the side yard, where her father's old crab traps and tools are kept. She knows there is a shovel in there. She knows where the key is.

The storm ends an hour before dawn, and she is ready.

It is her own death she is worried about, of course, not that of Theophile (whoever he may be). She is at the age where her curiosity about the weakness of the flesh out-weighs her fear of it. She thinks of him under the ground and she has to know whether he is really there. Has he ascended to Heaven or is he still in his grave, rotting? Whatever she finds, it cannot be worse than the thing she has imagined.

(So I think at the time.)

Rosalie is not feeling entirely sane as she eases out of the silent house, filches her father's shovel, and creeps through the dark village to the graveyard. She likes to go barefoot, and the soles of her feet are hard enough to walk over the broken edges of the glittering wet oyster-shells, but she knows you have to wear shoes after a heavy rain or worms might eat their way into your feet. So she slogs through the mud in her soaked sneakers, refusing to think about what she is going to do.

It is still too dark to see, but Rosalie knows her way by

heart through these village streets. Soon her hand finds the rusty iron gate of the graveyard, and it ratchets open at her touch. She winces at the harsh sound in the predawn silence, but there is no one around to hear.

At least, no one who can hear.

The crude silhouettes of headstones stab into the inky sky. Few families in the village can afford a carved marker; they lash two sticks together in the shape of a rough cross, or they hew their own stone out of granite if they can get a piece. Rosalie feels her way through a forest of jagged, irregular memorials to the dead. She knows some of them are only hand-lettered oak boards wedged into the ground. The shadows at the base of each marker are wet, shimmering. Foul mud sucks at her feet. She tells herself the smell is only stagnant water. In places the ground feels slick and lumpy; she cannot see what she is stepping on.

But when she comes near the stone she seeks, she can see it. For it is the finest stone in the graveyard, carved of moon-pale marble that seems to pull all light into its milky depths. His family had it made in New Orleans, spending what was probably their life's savings. The chiseled letters are as concise as razor cuts. Rosalie cannot see them, but she knows their every crevice and shadow. Only his name, stark and cold; no dates, no inscriptions, as if the family's grief was so great that they could not bear to say anything about him. Just inscribe it with his name and leave him there.

The plot of earth at the base of the stone is not visible, but she knows it all too well, a barren, muddy rectangle. There has been no time for grass or weeds to grow upon it; he has only been buried a fortnight, and the few sprouts that tried to come up have been beaten back down by the rain. But can he really be under there, shut up in a box, his lithe body bloating and bursting, his wonderful face and hands beginning to decay?

Rosalie steps forward, hand extended to touch the letters of his name: THEOPHILE THIBODEAUX. As she thinks – or dreams – the name, her fingers poised to trace its marble contours, an image fills her head, a jumble of sensations intense and erotic. A boy older than Rosalie, perhaps seventeen: a sharp pale face, too thin to be called handsome, but surely compelling; a curtain of long sleek black hair half-hiding eyes of fierce, burning azure. Theophile!

(All at once it is as if Rosalie's consciousness has merged completely with mine. My heart twists with a young girl's love and lust for this spitfire Cajun boy. I am dimly aware of Rosalie's drunken twenty-year-old body asleep on her bed, her feminine viscera twitching at the memory of him. O, how he touched her – O, how he tasted her!)

She had known it was wrong in the eyes of God. Her mama had raised her to be a good girl. But the evenings she had spent with Theophile after dances and church socials, sitting on an empty dock with his arm around her shoulders, leaning into the warm hollow of his chest – that could not be wrong. After a week of knowing her he had begun to show her the things he wrote on his ink-blackened relic of an Olympia typewriter, poems and stories, songs of the swamp. And that could not be wrong.

And the night they had sneaked out of their houses to meet, the night in the empty boathouse near Theophile's home – that could not be wrong either. They had begun only kissing, but the kisses grew too hot, too wild – Rosalie felt her insides boiling. Theophile answered her heat with his own. She felt him lifting the hem of her skirt and – carefully, almost reverently – sliding off her cotton panties. Then he was stroking the dark down between her legs, teasing her with the very tips of his fingers, rubbing faster and deeper until she felt like a blossom about to burst with sweet nectar. Then he parted her legs wider and bent to kiss her there as tenderly as he had kissed her mouth. His tongue was soft yet rough, like a soapy washcloth, and Rosalie had thought her young body would die with the pleasure of it. Then, slowly, Theophile was easing himself into her, and yes, she wanted him there, and yes, she was clutching at his back, pulling him farther in, refusing to heed the sharp pain of first entry. He rested inside her, barely moving; he lowered his head to kiss her sore developing nipples, and Rosalie felt the power of all womanhood shudder through her. This could not be wrong.

With the memories fixed firmly in her mind she takes another step toward his headstone. The ground crumbles away beneath her feet, and she falls headlong into her lover's grave.

The shovel whacks her across the spine. The rotten smell billows around her, heavy and ripe: spoiling meat, rancid fat, a sweetish-sickly odor. The fall stuns her. She struggles in the gritty muck, spits it out of her mouth.

Then the first pale light of dawn breaks across the sky, and Rosalie stares into the ruined face of Theophile.

(Now her memories flooded over me like the tide. Some time after they had started meeting in the boathouse she began to feel sick all the time; the heat made her listless. Her monthly blood, which had been coming for only a year, stopped. Mama took her into the next town to see a doctor, and he confirmed what Rosalie had already dreaded: she was going to have Theophile's baby.)

Her papa was not a hard man, nor cruel. But he had been raised in the bosom of the Church, and he had learned to measure his own worth by the honor of his family. Theophile never knew his Rosalie was pregnant. Rosalie's father waited for him in the boathouse one night. He stepped in holding a new sheaf of poems, and Papa's deer shot caught him across the chest and belly, a hundred tiny black eyes weeping red tears.

Papa was locked up in the county jail now and Mama said that soon he would go someplace even worse, someplace where they could never see him again. Mama said it wasn't Rosalie's fault, but Rosalie could see in her eyes that it was.

It has been the wettest spring anyone can remember, a month of steady rains. The water table in Louisiana bayou country is already so high that a hole will begin to draw water at a depth of two feet or less. All this spring the table has risen steadily, soaking the ground, drowning grass and flowers, making a morass of the sweet swamp earth. Cattails have sprung up at the edge of the graveyard. But the storm last night pushed the groundwater to saturation point and beyond. The wealthy folk of New Orleans bury their dead in vaults above ground to protect them from this very danger. But no one here can afford a marble vault, or even a brick one.

And the village graveyard has flooded at last.

Some of the things that have floated to the surface are little more than bone. Others are swollen to three or four times their size, gassy mounds of decomposed flesh rising like islands from the mud; some of these have silk flower petals stuck to them like obscene decorations. Flies rise lazily, then descend again in glittering, circling clouds. Here are mired the warped boards of coffins split open by the water's relentless pull. There floats the plaster figurine of a saint, his face and the color of his robes washed away by rain. Yawning eyeless faces thrust out of stagnant pools, seeming to gasp for breath. Rotting hands unfold like blighted tiger lilies. Every drop of water, every inch of earth in the graveyard is foul with the effluvium of the dead.

But Rosalie can only see the face thrust into hers, the body crushed beneath her own. Theophile's eyes have fallen back into their sockets and his mouth is open; his tongue is gone. She sees thin white worms teeming in the passage of his throat. His nostrils are widening black holes beginning to encroach upon the greenish flesh of his cheeks. His sleek hair is almost gone; the few strands left are thin and scummy, nibbled by waterbugs. (Sitting on the dock, Rosalie and Theophile used to spit into the water and watch the shiny black beetles swarm around the white gobs; Theophile had told her they would eat hair and toenails too.) In places she can see the glistening dome of his skull. *The skull behind the dear face; the skull that cradled the thoughts and dreams* . . .

She thinks of the shovel she brought and wonders what she meant to do with it. Did she *want* to see Theophile like this? Or had she really expected to find his grave empty, his fine young body gone fresh and whole to God?

No. She had only wanted to know where he was. Because she had nothing left of him – his family would give her no poems, no lock of hair. And now she had even lost his seed.

(The dogs ran Papa to earth in the swamp where he had hidden and the men dragged him off to jail. As they led him toward the police car, Theophile's mother ran up to him and spat in his face. Papa was handcuffed and could not wipe himself; he only stood there with the sour spit of sorrow running down his cheeks, and his eyes looked confused, as if he was unsure just what he had done.

Mama made Rosalie sleep in bed with her that night. But when Rosalie woke up the next morning Mama was gone; there was only a note saying she would be back before sundown. Sure enough, she straggled in with the afternoon's last light. She had spent the whole day in the swamp. Her face was scratched and sweaty, the cuffs of her jeans caked with mud.

Mama had brought back a basketful of herbs. She didn't fix dinner, but instead spent the evening boiling the plants down to a thin syrup. They exuded a bitter, stinging scent as they cooked. The potion sat cooling until the next night. Then Mama made Rosalie drink it all down.

It was the worst pain she had ever felt. She thought her intestines and her womb and the bones of her pelvis were being wrung in a giant merciless fist. When the bleeding started she thought her very insides were dissolving. There were thick clots and ragged shreds of tissue in the blood.

'It won't damage you,' Mama told her, 'and it will be over by morning.'

True to Mama's word, just before dawn Rosalie felt   37

something solid being squeezed out of her. She knew she was losing the last of Theophile. She tried to clamp the walls of her vagina around it, to keep him inside her as long as she could. But the thing was slick and formless, and it slid easily on to the towel Mama had spread between her legs. Mama gathered the towel up quickly and would not let Rosalie see what was inside.

Rosalie heard the toilet flush once, then twice. Her womb and the muscles of her abdomen felt as if they had gone through Mama's kitchen grater. But the pain was nothing compared to the emptiness she felt in her heart.

The sky is growing lighter, showing her more of the graveyard around her: the corpses borne on the rising water, the maggot-ridden mud. Theophile's face yawns into hers. Rosalie struggles against him and feels his sodden flesh give beneath her weight. She is beyond recognizing her love now. She is frantic; she fights him. Her hand strikes his belly and punches in up to the wrist.

Then suddenly Theophile's body opens like a flower made of carrion, and she sinks into him. Her elbows are trapped in the brittle cage of his ribs. Her face is pressed into the bitter soup of his organs. Rosalie whips her head to one side. Her face is a mask of putrescence. It is in her hair, her nostrils; it films her eyes. She is drowning in the body that once gave her sustenance. She opens her mouth to scream and feels things squirming in between her teeth.

'My *cherie* Rosalie,' she hears the voice of her lover whispering.

And then the rain pours down again.

Unpleasant.

I tore myself screaming from Rosalie – screaming silently, unwilling to wake her. In that instant I was afraid of her for what she had gone through; I dreaded to see her eyes snap open like a doll's, meeting me full in the face.

But Rosalie was only sleeping a troubled slumber. She muttered fitful disjointed words; there was a cold sheen of sweat on her brow; she exuded a flowery, powerful smell of sex. I hovered at the edge of the bed and studied her ringed hands clenched into small fists, her darting, jumping eyelids still stained with yesterday's makeup. I could only imagine the ensuing years and torments that had brought that little girl to this night, to this room. That had made her want to wear the false trappings of death, after having wallowed in the truth of it.

But I *knew* how difficult it would be to talk these memories out of her. There could be no consolation and no compensation for a past so cruel. No treasure, no matter how valuable, could matter in the face of such lurid terror.

So I assure you that the thing I did next was done out of pure mercy – not a desire for personal gain, or control over Rosalie. I had never done such a thing to her before. 39

She was my friend; I wished to deliver her from the poison of her memories. It was as simple as that.

I gathered up my courage and I went back into Rosalie's head. Back in through her eyes and the whorled tunnels of her ears, back into the spongy electric forest of her brain.

I cannot be more scientific than this: I found the connections that made the memory. I searched out the nerves and subtle acids that composed the dream, the morsels of Rosalie's brain that still held a residue of Theophile, the cells that were blighted by his death.

And I erased it all.

I pitied Theophile. Truly I did. There is no existence more lonely than death, especially a death where no one is left to mourn you.

But Rosalie belonged to me now.

I had her rent a boat.

It was easy for her to learn how to drive it: boating is in the Cajun blood. We made an exploratory jaunt or two down through Barataria – where two tiny hamlets much like Rosalie's home village, both bore my name – and I regaled a fascinated Rosalie with tales of burials at sea, of shallow bayou graves, of a rascal whose empty eye sockets dripped with Spanish moss.

When I judged her ready, I guided her to a spot I remembered well, a clearing where five enormous oaks grew from one immense, twisted trunk. The five sentinels, we called them in my day. The wind soughed in the upper branches. The swamp around us was hushed, expectant.

After an hour of digging, Rosalie's shiny new shovel unearthed the lid and upper portion of a great iron chest. Her brittle hair was stringy with sweat. Her black lace dress was caked with mud and clay. Her face had gone paler than usual with exertion; in the half-light of the swamp it was almost luminescent. She had never looked so beautiful to me as she did at that moment.

She stared at me. Her tired eyes glittered as if with fever.

'Open it,' I urged.

Rosalie swung the shovel at the heart-shaped hasp of the chest and knocked it loose on the first try. Once more and it fell away in a show of soggy rust. She glanced back at me once more – looking for what, I wonder; seeing what? – and then heaved open the heavy lid.

And the sixth sentinel sat up to greet her.

I always took an extra man along when I went into the swamp to bury treasure. One I didn't trust, or didn't need. He and my reliable henchmen would dig the hole and drag the chest to the edge of it, ready to heave in. Then I would gaze deep into the eyes of each man and ask, in a voice both quiet and compelling, 'Who wishes to guard my treasure?' My men knew the routine, and were silent. The extra man – currying favor as the useless and unreliable will do – always volunteered.

Then my top lieutenant would take three steps forward and put a ball in the lowly one's brain. His corpse was laid tenderly in the chest, his blood seeping into the mounds of gold or silver or glittering jewels, and I would tuck in one of my mojo bags, the ones I had specially made in New Orleans. Then the chest was sunk in the mire of the swamp, and my man, now rendered trustworthy, was left to guard my treasure until I should need it.

I was the only one who could open those chests. The combined magic of the mojo bag and the anger of the betrayed man's spirit saw to that.

My sixth sentinel wrapped skeletal arms around Rosalie's neck and drew her down. His jaws yawned wide and I saw teeth, still hungry after two hundred years, clamp down on her throat.

A mist of blood hung in the air; from the chest there was a ripping sound, then a noise of quick, choking agony. I hoped he would not make it too painful for her. After all, she was the woman I had chosen to spend eternity with.

I had told Rosalie that she would never again have to wriggle out of flimsy costumes under the eyes of slobbering men, and I had not lied. I had told her that she would never have to worry about money any more, and I had not lied. What I had neglected to tell her was that I did not wish to share my treasures – I only wanted her dead, my Hard-luck Rosalie, free from this world that pained her so, free to wander with me through the unspoiled swamps and bayous, through the ancient buildings of a city mired in time.

Soon Rosalie's spirit left her body and flew to me. It had nowhere else to go. I felt her struggling furiously against my love, but she would give in soon. I had no shortage of time to convince her.

I slipped my arm around Rosalie's neck and planted a kiss on her ectoplasmic lips. Then I clasped her wisp of a hand in mine, and we disappeared together.

Calcutta, Lord of Nerves

I was born in a north Calcutta hospital in the heart of an Indian midnight just before the beginning of the monsoon season. The air hung heavy as wet velvet over the Hooghly River, offshoot of the holy Ganga, and the stumps of banyan trees on the Upper Chitpur Road were flecked with dots of phosphorus like the ghosts of flames. I was as dark as the new moon in the sky, and I cried very little. I feel as if I remember this, because this is the way it must have been.

My mother died in labor, and later that night the hospital burned to the ground. (I have no reason to connect the two incidents; then again, I have no reason not to. Perhaps a desire to live burned on in my mother's heart. Perhaps the flames were fanned by her hatred for me, the insignificant mewling infant that had killed her.) A nurse carried me out of the roaring husk of the building and laid me in my father's arms. He cradled me, numb with grief.

My father was American. He had come to Calcutta five years earlier, on business. There he had fallen in love with my mother and, like a man who will not pluck a flower from its garden, he could not bear to see her removed from the hot, lush, squalid city that had spawned her. It was part of her exotica. So my father stayed in Calcutta. Now his flower was gone. He pressed his thin chapped lips to the satin of my hair. I remember opening my eyes – they felt tight and shiny, parched by the flames – and looking up at the column of smoke that roiled into the sky, a night sky blasted cloudy pink like a sky full of blood and milk.

There would be no milk for me, only chemical-tasting drops of formula from a plastic nipple. The morgue was in the basement of the hospital and did not burn. My mother lay on a metal table, a hospital gown stiff with her dying sweat pulled up over her red-smeared crotch and thighs. Her eyes stared up through the blackened skeleton of the hospital, up to the milky bloody sky, and ash filtered down to mask her pupils.

My father and I left for America before the monsoon came. Without my mother Calcutta was a pestilential hellhole, a vast cremation ground, or so my father thought. In America he could send me to school and movies, ball games and Boy Scouts, secure in the knowledge that someone else would take care of me or I would take care of myself. There were no *thuggees* to rob me and cut my throat, no *goondas* who would snatch me and sell my bones for fertilizer. There were no cows to infect the streets with their steaming sacred piss. My father could give me over to the comparative wholesomeness of

American life, leaving himself free to sit in his darkened bedroom and drink whisky until his long sensitive nose floated hazily in front of his face and the sabre edge of his grief began to dull. He was the sort of man who has only one love in his lifetime, and knows with the sick fervor of a fatalist that this love will be taken from him someday, and is hardly surprised when it happens.

When he was drunk he would talk about Calcutta. My little American mind rejected the place – I was in love with air-conditioning, hamburgers and pizza, the free and undiscriminating love that was lavished upon me every time I twisted the TV dial – but somewhere in my Indian heart I longed for it. When I turned eighteen and my father finally failed to wake up from one of his drunken stupors, I returned to the city of my bloody birth as soon as I had the plane fare in my hand.

Calcutta, you will say. What a place to have been when the dead began to walk.

And I reply, what better place to be? What better place than a city where five million people look as if they are already dead – might as well be dead – and another five million wish they were?

I have a friend named Devi, a prostitute who began her work at the age of fifteen from a tarpaper shack on Sudder Street. Sudder is the Bourbon Street of Calcutta, but there is far less of the carnival there, and no one wears a mask on Sudder Street because disguises are useless when shame is irrelevant. Devi works the big hotels now, selling American tourists or British expatriates or German businessmen a taste of exotic Bengal spice. She is gaunt and beautiful and hard as nails. Devi says the world is a whore, too, and Calcutta is the pussy of the world. The world squats and spreads its legs, and Calcutta is the dank sex you see revealed there, wet and fragrant with a thousand odors both delicious and foul. A source of lushest pleasure, a breeding ground for every conceivable disease.

The pussy of the world. It is all right with me. I like pussy, and I love my squalid city.

The dead like pussy too. If they are able to catch a woman and disable her enough so that she cannot resist, you will see the lucky ones burrowing in between her legs as happily as the most avid lover. They do not have to come up for air. I have seen them eat all the way up into the body cavity. The internal female organs seem to be a great delicacy, and why not? They are the caviar of the human body. It is a sobering thing to come across a woman sprawled in the gutter with her intestines sliding from the shredded ruin of her womb, but you do not react. You do not distract the dead from their repast. They are slow and stupid, but that is all the more reason for you to be smart and quick and quiet. They will do the same thing to a man – chew off the soft penis and scrotal sac like choice morsels of squid, leaving only a red raw hole. But you can sidle by while they are feeding and they will not notice you. I do not try to hide from them. I walk the streets and look; that is all I do anymore. I am fascinated. This is not horror, this is simply more of Calcutta.

First I would sleep late, through the sultry morning into the heat of the afternoon. I had a room in one of the decrepit marble palaces of the old city. Devi visited me here often, but on a typical morning I woke alone, clad only in twisted bedsheets and a luxurious patina of sweat. Sun came through the window and fell in bright bars across the floor. I felt safe in my second-story room as long as I kept the door locked. The dead were seldom able to navigate stairs, and they could not manage the sustained cooperative effort to break down a locked door. They were no threat to me. They fed upon those who had given up, those too traumatized to keep running: the senile, abandoned old, the catatonic young women who sat in gutters cradling babies that had died during the night. These were easy prey.

The walls of my room were painted a bright coral and the sills and door were aqua. The colors caught the sun and made the day seem cheerful despite the heat that shimmered outside. I went downstairs, crossed the empty courtyard with its dry marble fountain, and went out into the street. This area was barren in the heat, painfully bright, with parched weeds lining the road and an occasional smear of cow dung decorating the gutter. By nightfall both weeds and dung might be gone. Children collected cow shit and patted it into cakes held together with straw, which could be sold as fuel for cooking fires.

I headed toward Chowringhee Road, the broad main thoroughfare of the city. Halfway up my street, hunched under the awning of a mattress factory, I saw one of the catatonic young mothers. The dead had found her too. They had already taken the baby from her arms and eaten through the soft part at the top of the skull. Vacuous bloody faces rose and dipped. Curds of tender brain fell from slack mouths. The mother sat on the curb nearby, her arms cradling nothing. She wore a filthy green sari that was ripped across the chest. The woman's breasts protruded heavily, swollen with milk. When the dead finished with her baby they would start on her, and she would make no resistance. I had seen it before. I knew how the milk would spurt and then gush as they tore into her breasts. I knew how hungrily they would lap up the twin rivers of blood and milk.

Above their bobbing heads, the tin awning dripped long ropy strands of cotton. Cotton hung from the roof in dirty clumps, caught in the corners of the doorway like spiderweb. Someone's radio blared faintly in another part of the building, tuned to an English-language Christian broadcast. A gospel hymn assured Calcutta that its dead in Christ would rise. I moved on toward Chowringhee.

Most of the streets in the city are positively cluttered

with buildings. Buildings are packed in cheek-by-jowl, helter-skelter, like books of different sizes jammed into a rickety bookcase. Buildings even sag over the street so that all you see overhead is a narrow strip of sky crisscrossed by miles of clotheslines. The flapping silks and cottons are very bright against the sodden, dirty sky. But there are certain vantage points where the city opens up and all at once you have a panoramic view of Calcutta. You see a long muddy hillside that has become home to a *bustee*, thousands and thousands of slum dwellings where tiny fires are tended through the night. The dead come often to these slums of tin and cardboard, but the people do not leave the *bustee* – where would they go? Or you see a wasteland of disused factories, empty warehouses, blackened smokestacks jutting into a rust-colored sky. Or a flash of the Hooghly River, steel-gray in its shroud of mist, spanned by the intricate girder-and-wirescape of the Howrah Bridge.

Just now I was walking opposite the river. The waterfront was not considered a safe place because of the danger from drowning victims. Thousands each year took the long plunge off the bridge, and thousands more simply waded into the water. It is easy to commit suicide at a riverfront because despair collects in the water vapor. This is part of the reason for the tangible cloud of despair that hangs over Calcutta along with its veil of humidity.

50   Now the suicides and the drowned street children were

coming out of the river. At any moment the water might regurgitate one, and you would hear him scrabbling up the bank. If he had been in the water long enough he might tear himself to spongy gobbets on the stones and broken bricks that littered the waterfront; all that remained would be a trace of foul brown odor, like the smell of mud from the deep part of the river.

Police – especially the Sikhs, who are said to be more violent than Hindus – had been taking the dead up on the bridge to shoot them. Even from far away I could see spray-patterns of red on the drab girders. Alternatively they set the dead alight with gasoline and threw them over the railing into the river. At night it was not uncommon to see several writhing shapes caught in the downstream current, the fiery symmetry of their heads and arms and legs making them into five-pointed human stars.

I stopped at a spice vendor's stand to buy a bunch of red chrysanthemums and a handful of saffron. The saffron I had him wrap in a twist of scarlet silk. 'It is a beautiful day,' I said to him in Bengali. He stared at me, half amused, half appalled. 'A beautiful day for what?' True Hindu faith calls upon the believer to view all things as equally sacred. There is nothing profane – no dirty dog picking through the ash bin at a cremation ground, no stinking gangrenous stump thrust into your face by a beggar who seems to hold you personally responsible for all his woes. These things are as sacred as feasting day at 51 the holiest temple. But even for the most devout Hindus it has been difficult to see these walking dead as sacred. They are empty humans. That is the truly horrifying thing about them, more than their vacuous hunger for living flesh, more than the blood caked under their nails or the shreds of flesh caught between their teeth. They are soulless; there is nothing in their eyes; the sounds they make – their farts, their grunts and mewls of hunger – are purely reflexive. The Hindu, who has been taught to believe in the soul of everything, has a particular horror of these drained human vessels. But in Calcutta life goes on. The shops are still open. The confusion of traffic still inches its way up Chowringhee. No one sees any alternatives.

Soon I arrived at what was almost invariably my day's first stop. I would often walk twenty or thirty miles in a day – I had strong shoes and nothing to occupy my time except walking and looking. But I always began at the Kalighat, temple of the Goddess.

There are a million names for her, a million vivid descriptions: Kali the Terrible, Kali the Ferocious, skull-necklace, destroyer of men, eater of souls. But to me she was Mother Kali, the only one of the vast and colorful pantheon of Hindu gods that stirred my imagination and lifted my heart. She was the Destroyer, but all final refuge was found in her. She was the goddess of the age. She could bleed and burn and still rise again, very awake, beautifully terrible.

I ducked under the garlands of marigolds and strands of temple bells strung across the door, and I entered the temple of Kali. After the constant clamor of the street, the silence inside the temple was deafening. I fancied I could hear the small noises of my body echoing back to me from the ceiling far above. The sweet opium glaze of incense curled around my head. I approached the idol of Kali, the *jagrata.* Her gimlet eyes watched me as I came closer.

She was tall, gaunter and more brazenly naked than my friend Devi even at her best moments. Her breasts were tipped with blood – at least I always imagined them so – and her two sharp fangs and the long streamer of a tongue that uncurled from her open mouth were the color of blood too. Her hair whipped about her head and her eyes were wild, but the third crescent eye in the center of her forehead was merciful; it saw and accepted all.

The necklace of skulls circled the graceful stem of her neck, adorned the sculpted hollow of her throat. Her four arms were so sinuous that if you looked away even for an instant, they seemed to sway. In her four hands she held a noose of rope, a skull-staff, a shining sword, and a gaping, very dead-looking severed head. A silver bowl sat at the foot of the statue just beneath the head, where the blood from the neck would drip. Sometimes this was filled with goat's or sheep's blood as an offering. The bowl was full today. In these times the blood might well be human, though there was no putrid smell to indicate it had come from one of the dead.

I laid my chrysanthemums and saffron at Kali's feet. Among the other offerings, mostly sweets and bundles of spice, I saw a few strange objects. A fingerbone. A shrivelled mushroom of flesh that turned out upon closer inspection to be an ear. These were offerings for special protection, mostly wrested from the dead. But who was to say that a few devotees had not lopped off their own ears or finger joints to coax a boon from Kali? Sometimes when I had forgotten to bring an offering, I cut my wrist with a razor blade and let a few drops of my blood fall at the idol's feet.

I heard a shout from outside and turned my head for a moment. When I looked back, the four arms seemed to have woven themselves into a new pattern, the long tongue seemed to loll farther from the scarlet mouth. And – this was a frequent fantasy of mine – the wide hips now seemed to tilt forward, affording me a glimpse of the sweet and terrible petalled cleft between the thighs of the goddess.

I smiled up at the lovely sly face. 'If only I had a tongue as long as yours, Mother,' I murmured, 'I would kneel before you and lick the folds of your holy pussy until you screamed with joy.' The toothy grin seemed to grow wider, more lascivious. I imagined much in the presence of Kali.

Outside in the temple yard I saw the source of the
shout I had heard. There is a stone block upon which the

animals brought to Kali, mostly baby goats, are beheaded by the priests. A gang of roughly dressed men had captured a dead girl and were bashing her head in on the sacrificial block. Their arms rose and fell, ropy muscles flexing. They clutched sharp stones and bits of brick in their scrawny hands. The girl's half-pulped head still lashed back and forth. The lower jaw still snapped, though the teeth and bone were splintered. Foul thin blood coursed down and mingled with the rich animal blood in the earth beneath the block. The girl was nude, filthy with her own gore and waste. The flaccid breasts hung as if sucked dry of meat. The belly was burst open with gases. One of the men thrust a stick into the ruined gouge between the girl's legs and leaned on it with all his weight.

Only in extensive stages of decay can the dead be told from the lepers. The dead are greater in number now, and even the lepers look human when compared to the dead. But that is only if you get close enough to look into the eyes. The faces in various stages of wet and dry rot, the raw ends of bones rubbing through skin like moldy cheesecloth, the cancerous domes of the skulls are the same. After a certain point lepers could no longer stay alive begging in the streets, for most people would now flee in terror at the sight of a rotting face. As a result the lepers were dying, then coming back, and the two races mingled like some obscene parody of incest. Perhaps they actually could breed. The dead could obviously eat and digest, and seemed to excrete at random like everyone else in Calcutta, but I supposed no one knew whether they could ejaculate or conceive.

A stupid idea, really. A dead womb would rot to pieces around a fetus before it could come halfway to term; a dead scrotal sac would be far too cold a cradle for living seed. But no one seemed to know anything about the biology of the dead. The newspapers were hysterical, printing picture upon picture of random slaughter by dead and living alike. Radio stations had either gone off the air or were broadcasting endless religious exhortations that ran together in one long keening whine, the edges of Muslim, Hindu, Christian doctrine beginning to fray and blur.

No one in India could say for sure what made the dead walk. The latest theory I had heard was something about a genetically engineered microbe that had been designed to feed on plastic: a microbe that would save the world from its own waste. But the microbe had mutated and was now eating and 'replicating' human cells, causing basic bodily functions to reactivate. It did not much matter whether this was true. Calcutta was a city relatively unsurprised to see its dead rise and walk and feed upon it. It had seen them doing so for a hundred years.

All the rest of the lengthening day I walked through the city. I saw no more dead except a cluster far away at the
end of a blocked street, in the last rags of bloody light,

fighting each other over the bloated carcass of a sacred cow.

My favorite place at sunset is by the river where I can see the Howrah Bridge. The Hooghly is painfully beautiful in the light of the setting sun. The last rays melt onto the water like hot *ghee*, turning the river from steel to khaki to nearly golden, a blazing ribbon of light. The bridge rises black and skeletal into the fading orange sky. Tonight an occasional skirl of bright flowers and still-glowing greasy embers floated by, the last earthly traces of bodies cremated farther up the river. Above the bridge were the burning *ghats* where families lined up to incinerate their dead and cast the ashes into the holy river. Cremation is done more efficiently these days, or at least more hurriedly. People can reconcile in their hearts their fear of strangers' dead, but they do not want to see their own dead rise. I walked along the river for a while. The wind off the water carried the scent of burning meat. When I was well away from the bridge, I wandered back into the maze of narrow streets and alleyways that lead toward the docks in the far southern end of the city. People were already beginning to settle in for the night, though here a bedroom might mean your own packing crate or your own square of sidewalk. Fires glowed in nooks and corners.

A warm breeze still blew off the river and sighed its way through the winding streets. It seemed very late now. As I made my way from corner to corner, through intermittent pools of light and much longer patches of darkness, I heard small bells jingling to the rhythm of my footsteps. The brass bells of rickshaw men, ringing to tell me they were there in case I wished for a ride. But I could see none of the men. The effect was eerie, as if I were walking alone down an empty nighttime street being serenaded by ghostly bells. The feeling soon passed. You are never truly alone in Calcutta.

A thin hand slid out of the darkness as I passed. Looking into the doorway it came from, I could barely make out five gaunt faces, five forms huddled against the night. I dropped several coins into the hand and it slid out of sight again. I am seldom begged from. I look neither rich nor poor, but I have a talent for making myself all but invisible. People look past me, sometimes right through me. I don't mind; I see more things that way. But when I am begged from I always give. With my handful of coins, all five of them might have a bowl of rice and lentils tomorrow.

A bowl of rice and lentils in the morning, a drink of water from a broken standpipe at night.

It seemed to me that the dead were among the best-fed citizens of Calcutta.

Now I crossed a series of narrow streets and was surprised to find myself coming up behind the Kalighat. The side streets are so haphazardly arranged that you are

constantly finding yourself in places you had no idea you

were even near. I had been to the Kalighat hundreds of times, but I had never approached it from this direction. The temple was dark and still. I had not been here at this hour before, did not even know whether the priests were still here or if one could enter so late. But as I walked closer I saw a little door standing open at the back. The entrance used by the priests, perhaps. Something flickered from within: a candle, a tiny mirror sewn on a robe, the smoldering end of a stick of incense.

I slipped around the side of the temple and stood at the door for a moment. A flight of stone steps led up into the darkness of the temple. The Kalighat at night, deserted, might have been an unpleasant prospect to some. The thought of facing the fierce idol alone in the gloom might have made some turn away from those steps. I began to climb them.

The smell reached me before I ascended halfway. To spend a day walking through Calcutta is to be assailed by thousands of odors both pleasant and foul: the savor of spices frying in *ghee*, the stink of shit and urine and garbage, the sick-sweet scent of the little white flowers called *mogra* that are sold in garlands and that make me think of the gardenia perfume American undertakers use to mask the smell of their corpses.

Almost everyone in Calcutta is scrupulously clean in person, even the very poor. They will leave their trash and their spit everywhere, but many of them wash their bodies 59 twice a day. Still, everyone sweats under the sodden veil of heat, and at midday any public place will be redolent with the smell of human perspiration, a delicate tang like the mingled juices of lemons and onions. But lingering in the stairwell was an odor stronger and more foul than any I had encountered today. It was deep and brown and moist; it curled at the edges like a mushroom beginning to dry. It was the perfume of mortal corruption. It was the smell of rotting flesh.

Then I came up into the temple, and I saw them.

The large central room was lit only with candles that flickered in a restless draft, first this way, then that. In the dimness the worshippers looked no different from any other supplicants at the feet of Kali. But as my eyes grew accustomed to the candlelight, details resolved themselves. The withered hands, the ruined faces. The burst body cavities where ropy organs could be seen trailing down behind the cagework of ribs.

The offerings they had brought.

By day Kali grinned down upon an array of blossoms and sweetmeats lovingly arranged at the foot of her pedestal. The array spread there now seemed more suited to the goddess. I saw human heads balanced on raw stumps of necks, eyes turned up to crescents of silver-white. I saw gobbets of meat that might have been torn from a belly or a thigh. I saw severed hands like pale lotus flowers, the fingers like petals opening silently in the night.

60

Most of all, piled on every side of the altar, I saw bones. Bones picked so clean that they gleamed in the candlelight. Bones with smears of meat and long snotty runners of fat still attached. Skinny arm-bones, clubby leg-bones, the pretzel of a pelvis, the beadwork of a spine. The delicate bones of children. The crumbling ivory bones of the old. The bones of those who could not run.

These things the dead brought to their goddess. She had been their goddess all along, and they her acolytes.

Kali's smile was hungrier than ever. The tongue lolled like a wet red streamer from the open mouth. The eyes were blazing black holes in the gaunt and terrible face. If she had stepped down from her pedestal and approached me now, if she had reached for me with those sinuous arms, I might not have been able to fall to my knees before her. I might have run. There are beauties too terrible to be borne.

Slowly the dead began to turn toward me. Their faces lifted and the rotting cavities of their nostrils caught my scent. Their eyes shone iridescent. Faint starry light shimmered in the empty spaces of their bodies. They were like cutouts in the fabric of reality, like conduits to a blank universe. The void where Kali ruled and the only comfort was in death.

They did not appoach me. They stood holding their precious offerings and they looked at me – those of them that still had eyes – or they looked through me. At that moment I felt more than invisible. I felt empty enough to belong among these human shells.

A ripple seemed to pass through them. Then – in the uncertain candlelight, in the light that shimmered from the bodies of the dead – Kali did move.

The twitch of a finger, the deft turn of a wrist – at first it was so slight as to be nearly imperceptible. But then her lips split into an impossibly wide, toothy grin and the tip of her long tongue curled. She rotated her hips and swung her left leg high into the air. The foot that had trod on millions of corpses made a *pointe* as delicate as a prima ballerina's. The movement spread her sex wide open.

But it was not the petalled mandala-like cleft I had imagined kissing earlier. The pussy of the goddess was an enormous deep red hole that seemed to lead down to the center of the world. It was a gash in the universe, it was rimmed in blood and ash. Two of her four hands beckoned toward it, inviting me in. I could have thrust my head into it, then my shoulders. I could have crawled all the way into that wet crimson eternity, and kept crawling forever.

Then I did run. Before I had even decided to flee I found myself falling down the stone staircase, cracking my head and my knee on the risers. At the bottom I was up and running before I could register the pain. I told myself that I thought the dead would come after me. I do not know what I truly feared was at my back. At times I thought I was running not away from something, but toward it.

I ran all night. When my legs grew too tired to carry me I would board a bus. Once I crossed the bridge and found myself in Howrah, the even poorer suburb on the other side of the Hooghly. I stumbled through desolate streets for an hour or more before doubling back and crossing over into Calcutta again. Once I stopped to ask for a drink of water from a man who carried two cans of it slung on a long stick across his shoulders. He would not let me drink from his tin cup, but poured a little water into my cupped hands. In his face I saw the mingled pity and disgust with which one might look upon a drunk or a beggar. I was a well-dressed beggar, to be sure, but he saw the fear in my eyes.

In the last hour of the night I found myself wandering through a wasteland of factories and warehouses, of smokestacks and rusty corrugated tin gates, of broken windows. There seemed to be thousands of broken windows. After a while I realized I was on the Upper Chitpur Road. I walked for a while in the watery light that fills the sky before dawn. Eventually I left the road and staggered through the wasteland. Not until I saw its girders rising around me like the charred bones of a prehistoric animal did I realize I was in the ruins of the hospital where I had been born.

The hole of the basement had filled up with broken glass and crumbling metal, twenty years' worth of cinders and weeds, all washed innocent in the light of the breaking dawn. Where the building had stood there was only a vast depression in the ground, five or six feet deep. I slid down the shallow embankment, rolled, and came to rest in the ashes. They were infinitely soft; they cradled me. I felt as safe as an embryo. I let the sunrise bathe me. Perhaps I had climbed into the gory chasm between Kali's legs after all, and found my way out again.

Calcutta is cleansed each morning by the dawn. If only the sun rose a thousand times a day, the city would always be clean.

Ashes drifted over me, smudged my hands gray, flecked my lips. I lay safe in the womb of my city, called by its poets Lord of Nerves, city of joy, the pussy of the world. I felt as if I lay among the dead. I was that safe from them: I knew their goddess, I shared their many homes. As the sun came up over the mud and glory of Calcutta, the sky was so full of smoky clouds and pale pink light that it seemed, to my eyes, to burn.

How to Get Ahead in New York

Consider this scene:

Four a.m. in the Port Authority bus terminal, New York City. The Port Authority is a bad place at the best of times, a place where Lovecraft's wrong geometry might well hold sway. The master of purple prose maintained that the human mind could be driven mad by contemplation of angles subtly skewed, of other planes where the three corners of a triangle might add up to less than a hundred and eighty degrees, or to more.

Such is the Port Authority: even in the bustle of midday, corners do not appear to meet up quite right; corridors seem to slope from one end to the other. Even in full daylight, the Port Authority terminal is a bad place. At five a.m. it is wholly soulless.

Consider two young men just off a Greyhound from North Carolina. They were not brothers, but they might be thought brothers, although they looked nothing alike: it was suggested in the way the taller one, crow-black hair shoved messily behind his ears, kept close to his fairhaired companion as if protecting him. It was implied in the way they looked around the empty terminal and then glanced at each other, exchanging bad impressions without saying 65 a word. They were not brothers, but they had known each other since childhood, and neither had ever been to New York before.

The corridor was flooded with dead fluorescent light. They had seen an EXIT sign pointing this way, but the corridor ended in a steel door marked NO ADMITTANCE. Should anyone find this message ambiguous, a heavy chain had been looped through the door handle and snapped shut with a padlock as large as a good-sized fist.

The fair boy turned around in a complete circle, lifted his head and flared his nostrils. His pale blue eyes slipped halfway shut, the lids fluttering. His friend watched him warily. After a minute he came out of it, shook himself a little, still nervous. 'I don't like it here, Steve. I can't find my way anywhere.'

Steve didn't like it either, wished they could have avoided the terminal altogether. They'd planned to drive up, but Steve's old T-bird had developed an alarming engine knock which threatened to become a death rattle if not dealt with kindly. The trip was all planned; they were booked to play at a club in the East Village – but they also meant to embark on a cross-country road trip next month. Steve left the car with his mechanic, telling him to fix it or scrap the mother-fucker, Steve didn't care which. Ghost stood by half-smiling, listening to this exchange. Then, while Steve was still bitching, he had walked up the street to the Farmers Hardware store that doubled as Missing

Mile's bus station and charged two round-trip tickets to his credit card. He hated using that card, hated the feel of the thing in his pocket, but this surely counted as an emergency. That same night they were New York–bound.

'It's just the damn *bus station*,' Steve said. 'You ever know a town that could be judged by its bus station?' But as usual, there was no use arguing with Ghost's intuition. The place set Steve's teeth on edge too.

Ghost hitched his backpack up on his shoulder. They turned away from the padlocked door and tried to retrace their steps, but every corridor seemed to lead further into the bowels of the place. The soft sound of Ghost's sneakers and the sharp clatter of Steve's bootheels echoed back at them: *shush–clop, shush–clop.* Through Ghost's thin T-shirt Steve saw the sharp winglike jut of his shoulderblades, the shadowed knobs of his spine. The strap of the backpack pulled Ghost's shirt askew; his pale hair straggled silkily over his bare, sweaty neck. Steve carried only a guitar case, the instrument inside padded with a spare shirt and a few extra pairs of socks.

They came to another dead end, then to the motionless hulk of an escalator with a chain strung across its railings. A KEEP OUT sign hung from the chain, swinging lazily as if someone had given it a push and then ducked out of sight just before Steve and Ghost came around the corner. Steve began to feel like a stupid hick, to feel like the place was playing tricks on them. *Came to the Big City and* 67 *couldn't even find our way out of the bus station. We ought to sit down right here and wait for the next bus headed south, and when it comes, we ought to hop on it and go right back home. Fuck New York, fuck the big club date. I don't like it here either.*

But that was stupid. The city was out there somewhere, and it had to get better than this.

Port Authority, Ghost decided, was about the worst place he had ever been in. Everything about it looked wrong, smelled wrong, leaned wrong. There were patterns on the floor made by the grime of a thousand soles; there was a bloody handprint on the tile wall. Looking at it, Ghost tried to close off his mind: he didn't want to know how it had gotten there. He managed to block out all but a faint impression of dirty knuckles plowing into a soft toothless mouth.

All at once the corridors shook and shuddered. The floor vibrated beneath his feet, throwing Ghost off balance. He had no way of knowing that this loss of equilibrium was caused by the subways constantly passing through; it made him feel as if the place were trying to digest him.

How did you ever get here? he thought. *How did you get from the green mountains, from the kudzu traintracks and the lazy hot summers, all the way to this city that could chew you up and spit you out like a wad of gum that's lost its flavor? How did you get to this place where you can never* 68 *belong?*

Immersed in his thoughts, he had let Steve get a little ahead of him. He looked up an instant before the apparition of death reeled around the corner; he heard Steve's curse, the sharp '*Fuck!*' that was nearly a gag, as the apparition lurched into Steve.

Steve's arms shot out reflexively, found the man's shoulders and shoved him away. The bum fell back against the wall, leaving a long wet smear on the tiles. His ragged suit jacket and the wattles of his throat were webbed with pale stringy vomit that dripped off his chin and made small foul splatters on the floor. His skin was gray, flaccid. It made Ghost think of a pumpkin that had sat too long in his grandmother's cellar once, waiting for Halloween; when he'd poked it, his finger had punched through the rind and sunk into the soft rotten meat. This man's skin looked as if it would rupture just as easily. One of his eyes was filmed over with a creamy yellowish cataract. The other eye listed toward the ceiling, watered and seemed about to spill over, then managed to track. When the eye met his, Ghost felt ice tingle along his spine. There was no one home behind that eye.

A wasted claw of a hand came up clutching a Styrofoam cup in which a few coins rattled. Veins stood out on the back of the hand. In the dead light they were stark and clear as a map of the man's ruined soul. 'Spare change for my li'l girl,' he muttered. His voice caught in his throat, then dragged itself out slow as a bad recording. 'My li'l girl's sick. Gotta catch the mornin' bus to Jersey.'

Ghost looked at Steve. The understanding passed clearly between them: *bullshit.* There was no little girl in Jersey, there was nothing waiting for this man except the love at the bottom of a bottle. But the reality of him staggering through the desolate corridors in his vomit-caked coat, with his lone empty eye – that was worse than any sob story. Steve pulled out his wallet; Ghost dug through the pockets of his army jacket. They came up with a dollar each and stuffed the bills into the broken Styrofoam cup.

The bum threw his head back and a weird hooting sound came from his cracked lips. It was not quite a word, not quite a whistle. It reverberated off the tiles and ceilings.

And then the walls and the corridors of the Port Authority seemed to split wide open, and the legions of the hopeless spilled forth.

The bums were everywhere at once, coming from every direction, their eyes fixed on Steve's wallet and Ghost's open hands and the crisp bills poking out of the cup. Most of them had their own jingling cups; they shoved them at Steve, at Ghost, and their eyes implored. Their voices rose in a hundred meaningless pleas: *cuppa coffee . . . sick baby . . . hungry, mister, I'm hungry.* In the end the voices only meant one thing. *Give me. You who have, when I have none – give me.*

They kept coming. There seemed to be no end to them.

Their hands reached for the money and grasped it. A persistent young brother grabbed a handful of Steve's hair and wouldn't let go until Steve reared back and punched him full in the face. He got a fistful of snot and ropy saliva for his trouble. As the boy fell away, Steve saw angry red holes in the pale flesh of his outstretched palms: needle marks. *He was my age*, Steve thought wildly; something in the eyes made him think the kid might have been even younger than twenty-four. *But he was already worn out enough to shoot up in the palms of his hands.*

Steve found himself flashing on *Dawn of the Dead*, a movie that had terrified him when he was a kid. He'd seen it again a couple of years ago and been surprised by how funny it really was: Romero's allegory of zombies roaming a modern mega-mall had escaped him at twelve. But now the original kid-terror flooded back. This was how it would be when the zombies ate you. They weren't very smart or quick, but there were a *lot* of them, and they would just keep coming and coming until you couldn't fight them any more.

Filth-caked nails scraped his flesh. The wallet was torn out of his grasp and dumped on the floor. Steve saw dirty hands shuffling through the trivia of his life. His driver's license. Ticket stubs from concerts he'd seen. A tattered review of Lost Souls?, his and Ghost's band, that had been written up in a Raleigh newspaper. Rage exploded like a crimson rocket in his brain. He had *worked* to get that money; he had *worked* to have a life, not see it trickle away from him like vomit on a dirty bus-station floor.

He hefted the guitar case – none of them seemed interested in that – and swung it in a wild arc. It connected with flesh, filthy hair, bone. Steve winced as he heard the jangling protest of the strings. He'd hit the first bum in his vomit-caked jacket, the only one they had willingly given money. *Try that for a handout, mother-fucker.* The bum fell to his knees, clutching the back of his skull. Even the blood welling up between his fingers had an unhealthy look, like the watery blood at the bottom of a meat tray. It spattered the dirty floor in large uneven drops.

Ghost was grappling for his backpack. An old woman with skin like spoiled hamburger pulled at one shoulder-strap. The buttons of her flannel shirt had popped open and her shrivelled breasts tumbled out. The nipples were long and leathery as the stems of mushrooms. Her hair was a uniform grayish-yellow mat overlaid with a layer of white gauze which seemed to thicken, to form dense little balls, in several spots. Networks of delicate threads led away from these; dark shapes moved sluggishly within them. *Cocoons*, Steve realized sickly. *She has cocoons in her hair.*

He grabbed the woman by the shoulders and shoved her away. Ghost's notebooks were in that backpack – the lyrics to every song they had written. Ghost's eyes met Steve's, pale blue gone darker with panic.

72

Then, for no discernible reason, the creeps began to lift their heads and scent the air. A silent alarm seemed to pass among them. One by one they shrank away, sidled along the walls and disappeared like wraiths into the maze of corridors. The money in their Styrofoam cups rustled and jingled. Steve thought of cockroaches scuttling for cover when the kitchen light snaps on. In less than a minute they were gone.

Steve and Ghost stared at each other, sweating, catching their breaths. Ghost held up a shaky hand. The cocoon lady's nails had left a long, shallow scratch along the back of it, from his knuckles to the bony knob of his wrist. A moment later they heard heavy, measured footsteps approaching. They edged closer together but did not otherwise react; this was surely the soul of the city itself coming to claim them.

The cop came around the corner all hard-edged and polished and gleaming, stopped at the sight of them, saw Steve's wallet and its contents scattered on the floor, frowned. His face was broad, Italian-looking, freshly shaved but the beard beneath the skin already showing faintly blue-black. 'Help you with something?' he asked, his voice sharp with suspicion.

Steve drew in a long trembling breath and Ghost spoke quickly, before Steve could. Cussing cops was never a good idea, no matter where you were. 'I think we got a little lost,' he said. 'Could you tell us how to get out of here?' 73

He was relieved when the cop pointed them in the right direction and Steve bent and scooped up his wallet, then stalked off without a word. Ghost's brain still ached from the long bus ride and the attack of the homeless people — or the people who lived, perhaps, in Port Authority. Worse than their grasping hands had been the touch of their minds upon his, as many-legged and hungry as mosquitoes. Their raw pain, the stink of their dead dreams. On top of that he hadn't needed Steve to get himself arrested. But Ghost was used to being the occasional peacemaker between Steve and almost everyone they knew. Steve bristled and Ghost calmed; that was just the way things were.

The sky was already brightening when they came out of the bus terminal. The city soared around them, bathed in a clear lavender light. The first building Ghost saw was an old stone church; the second was a four-story sex emporium, its neon shimmering pale pink in the dawn. Steve leaned back against the glass doors and began to laugh.

'Good morning, Hell's Kitchen,' he said.

Washington Square Park was in full regalia, though it was still early afternoon.

There were street musicians of every stripe, rappers clicking fast fingers and rattling heavy gold chains, old hippies with battered guitars and homemade pan pipes and permanent stoned smirks, young hippies singing solemn folk lyrics *a capella*, even a Dixieland brass band near the great stone arch. There was the savory mustard chili tang of hot dogs, the harsh smoulder of city exhaust, the woodsy smell of ganja burning. There were homeboys and Rasta men and hairy-chested drag queens, slumming yuppies and street freaks. There were the folks for whom every day was Halloween, faces painted pale, lips slashed crimson or black, ears and wrists decorated with silver crucifixes, skulls, charms of death and hoodoo. They huddled into their dark clothes, plucked at their dyed, teased, tortured hair, cut their black-rimmed eyes at passersby. There were punks in leather; there were drug dealers chanting the charms of their wares (*clean crystal ... sweetest smoke in the city ... goooood ice, gooooood blow*). There were cops on the beat, cops looking the other way.

And, of course, there were two white boys from North Carolina whose feet had just this morning touched New York City asphalt for the first time.

They had drunk vile coffee from a stand in Times Square, then walked around for a while. They kept losing track of the Empire State Building, which was the only landmark they recognized. The tranquil light of early morning soon gave way to the hustle and shove of the day. The air came alive with shouts, blaring horns, the constant low thrum of the city-machine.

Eventually – as soon as they could stand to go below

street-level again – they descended into the subway at Penn Station and didn't get out again until the Washington Square stop. At that point Ghost swore he would never enter a transit station or board any subway in New York City or anywhere else, ever again. It wasn't the crowds; since Port Authority the only panhandlers they'd seen had been shaking discreet cups or quietly noodling on saxophones. No one else had bothered them. It was the merciless white light in the stations and the bleak garbage-strewn deadliness of the tracks and the great clattering ratcheting roar of the trains. It was hurtling through sections of tunnel where the tracks split in two at the last heartstopping second before you smashed into solid stone. It was the abandoned tunnels that split off like dead universes. The very idea of the trains worming along beneath the city, in their honeycombed burrows, seemed horribly organic.

But topside, he was fine. Ghost found himself liking the stew of sounds and smells that comprised the city, and the colorful variety of the minds that brushed his, and the carnival of Washington Square. Steve stopped to watch the Dixieland band, and Ghost listened to the dipping, soaring brass for several minutes too.

But in his peripheral vision a man was rooting in a garbage can. He tried not to look, but couldn't help himself as the man pulled out a whole dripping chilidog, 76 brushed flies away, and bit into it.

The man was old and white, with long gray dreadlocks and mummified hands and the universal costume of the drifter, army jacket, baggy pants, Salvation Army shirt that just missed being a rag: an ensemble ready to fade into the background at a moment's notice. The chilidog was a carnage of ketchup and pickle relish and flaccid meat, the bun limp, sponge-soggy. The man's face registered more pleasure than distaste. The dog might taste awful, but there was still warm sun on his shoulders and a half-full bottle in his pocket and a goddamn huge party going on right here, right now. His eyes were curiously clear, almost childlike.

But it was garbage, he was eating garbage. The wire trashcan was crammed with ripening refuse. A redolent juice seeped out at the bottom, a distillation of every disgusting fluid in the can, moonshine for bluebottle flies. Ghost felt his mind stretching, trying to accommodate something he had never had to think closely about before. There were poor people in Missing Mile, sure. Most of the old men who played checkers outside the Farmers Hardware store were on some kind of government or military pension. Lots of people got food stamps. But were there people eating out of garbage cans? Were there people so desperate that they would band together and attack you for the change in your pocket?

You bet there are. They're everywhere. Your life has been just sheltered enough, just sanitized enough, that you didn't 77 *see them. But you can't get away from it here ... this city chews up its young and spits them back in your face.*

Ghost looked up, startled. He wasn't sure what had just happened; it felt as if the world, for an instant, had split and then reconverged. As if someone had had the exact same thought as him, at the exact same time.

He saw a young black man leaning on the low concrete wall nearby, also watching the old drifter. The young man was handsome, trendily barbered, dressed in casual but expensive-looking sport clothes. He wore gold-rimmed glasses with little round lenses, carried a radio Walkman in his breast pocket and a copy of *Spy* tucked under his arm. In his face as he watched the old man chewing was an ineffable sadness, not quite sympathy, not quite pity.

The hearts that would swell with rage back home — if you could call them hearts — to see a black man looking upon a white man with anything resembling pity ...

(Get outta that garbage, boy.)

The man shifted on the wall and looked straight at Ghost, warm mocha eyes meeting startled pale blue. And suddenly Ghost knew many things about this man. He was from a tiny town in south Georgia – Ghost didn't get the name – and his family had been crushingly poor. Not trash-eating poor ... but there had been a man in the town who was. Ancient and alone, black as midnight, brains pickled by half a century of rotgut wine. He was a no-town hobo of the sort people laughed at but looked out for; he had no colorful nickname, no family, no history. He was a smelly old wino who pissed his pants, and most of the whites in town, if they were aware of him at all, called him Hey Boy. As in *Hey, Boy, get outta that garbage.* As in *Hey, Boy, I'm talkin' to you.* As in *Hey, Boy, get off my property before I blow your nigger guts to Hell.*

And this young man, as a hungry scrawny child in this stagnant backwater of a town, had seen that happen.

Ghost saw the blood exploding through the air, smelled flame and cordite, redneck sweat and the raw sewage odor of Hey Boy's ruptured, blasted guts. He felt the giddy terror of a child hiding – where – he couldn't get it – viewing death up close for the first time, afraid its twin black barrels would swing his way next. He could not move, could not look away from the young man's calm brown eyes, until Steve touched his shoulder. 'Somebody just gave me directions to the club. It's real near here. You want to go check it out?'

Ghost glanced back over his shoulder as they left the park. The young man was no longer looking at him, and Ghost felt no urge to speak. They had already had the most intimate contact possible; of what use were words?

They crossed a wide traffic-filled avenue and turned east. Ghost wasn't sure just where the Village began, but the streets seemed to be getting narrower, the window displays more fabulous, the crowds decidedly funkier. 79

People wore silver studs in their noses, delicate hoops through their lips and eyebrows. A boy in a black fishnet shirt had both nipples pierced, with a filigree chain connecting the rings. There were shaved and painted scalps, long snaky braids, leather jackets jangling with zippers and buckles, flowing hippie dresses of gossamer and gauze. The streets of the East Village by day seemed a shrine to mutant fashion.

Steve pulled a joint from his sock, lit up, took a deep drag and passed it to Ghost. Ghost grabbed the burning cigarette and cupped it gingerly between his palms, trying to hide it, expecting a big cop hand to fall on his shoulder at any second. 'Are you *crazy?*'

Steve shook his head, then blew out a giant plume of smoke. 'It's cool. Terry said you could smoke right on the street up here, as long as you're discreet. He gave me this as a going-away present.'

Terry owned the record store where Steve worked, and was the best-travelled and most worldly of their crowd; also the biggest stoner, so he ought to know. But Ghost could not stretch his definition of *discreet* to include walking down one of the busiest streets in New York City with a cloud of pot smoke trailing behind. Still ... He looked thoughtfully at the joint in his hand, then brought it up to his lips and took a cautious toke. The spicy green flavor filled his throat, swirled through his lungs and his brain. New York probably imported every exotic strain of reefer from every country in the world, but Southern homegrown had to beat them all.

A few blocks later the crowds thinned out. The streets here felt older, grayer, somehow more soothing. More like a place where you could actually live. There were little groceries on every block with wooden stands of flowers and produce in front. Ghost smelled ginger and ripe tomatoes, the subtle cool scent of ice, the tang of fresh greens and herbs. Sage, basil, onions, thyme, sweet rosemary and soapy-smelling coriander. As long as he could smell herbs he was happy.

New York, Steve decided, was a city bent upon providing its citizens with plenty of food and information. In other parts of the city there had been hot dog carts everywhere, pizza parlors and cappuccino shops, restaurants serving food from Thailand, Mongolia, Latino-China, and everywhere else in the world; news-stands on every corner carried hundreds of papers, magazines, and often a wide selection of hardcore porn. There were radios and TVs blaring, headlines shrieking. In the first part of the Village Steve had seen more restaurants, comics shops, and several intriguing bookstores he planned to check out later. Here you had the little groceries, though not quite so many restaurants. For information, there were the street vendors.

Steve had started noticing them a while back, though he'd been too busy noticing everything else to pay much attention at first. But here they were more frequent and less obscured by the flow of the crowd. They set up tables or spread out army blankets, then arranged the stuff they wanted to sell and sat down to wait until somebody bought it. There were tables of ratty paperbacks, boxes of old magazines, tie-dyed T-shirts and ugly nylon buttpacks, cheap watches and household appliances laid out on the sidewalk like the leftovers from somebody's yard sale.

But as they walked farther, the wares started to get a little strange. At first it was just stuff that no one could possibly want, like a box of broken crayon-ends or a shampoo bottle filled with sand. Then they passed a man selling what looked like medical equipment: bedpans in a dusty row, unidentifiable tubes and pouches, some jar-shaped humps covered with a tattered army blanket. In the center of his display was a single artificial leg that had once been painted a fleshy pink. Now the paint was chipped, the limb's surface webbed with a thousand tiny, grimy cracks. The toeless foot was flat and squared-off, little more than a block of wood. At the top was a nightmarish jumble of straps and braces meant, Steve supposed, to hold the leg onto a body. He could not imagine walking around on such a thing every day.

'Where is this club?' Ghost asked nervously.

'Well ... I know we're near it.' Steve stopped at the corner, shoved sweaty hair out of his face, and looked around hoping the place would appear. 'The guy who gave me directions said it would be hard to find in the daytime. We're supposed to look for an unlit neon sign that says *Beware*.'

'Great.'

'WHAT PLACE YEZ LOOKIN' FOR?' boomed a voice behind them. It took Steve several seconds to realize that the vendor had spoken and was now motioning them over.

'Yez look like gentlemen in search of the unusual,' the vendor told them before they could say anything about clubs or directions. He was a white man of indeterminate age, dishwater-brown hair thin on top but straggling halfway down his back in an untidy braid. His eyes were hidden behind black wraparound shades, his grin as sharp and sudden as a razor. Steve noticed a strange ring on the second finger of the guy's right hand: a bird skull cast in silver, some species with huge hollow eyesockets and a long, tapering, lethal-looking beak that jutted out over the knuckle. It was lovely, but it also looked like a good tool for putting an eye out or ventilating a throat.

'Well, right now we're looking for this club –'

'Something UNUSUAL,' the vendor overrode. 'A collector's item maybe.' His hand hovered over his wares, straightened tubes and straps, caressed the artificial leg. 'Something yez don't see every day.' His face went immobile, then split back into that sharp crazy grin. 'Or rather – something yez DO see every day, but most of the time yez can't take the fuckers HOME WITH YA!'

His hand twitched back the army blanket covering the jar-shaped humps. A small cloud of dust rose into the air. Sunlight winked on polished glass. Steve cussed, took two steps back, then came forward again and bent to look.

Ghost, who had never in his life felt so far from home, burst into tears.

The man had six big glass jars arranged in two neat rows, sealed at the tops and filled with what could only be formaldehyde. Inside each jar, suspended in the murky liquid, was a large, pale, bloated shape: an undeniably real human head.

The necks appeared to have been surgically severed. Ghost could see layers of tissue within the stumps as precisely delineated as the circles of wood inside a tree trunk. One head was tilted far enough to the side to show a neat peg of bone poking from the meat of the neck. Several had shaved scalps; one had dark hair that floated and trailed like seaweed. Parts of faces were pressed flat against the glass: an ear, a swollen nostril, a rubbery lip pulled askew. Blood-suffused eyeballs protruded from their sockets like pickled hard-boiled eggs.

'How much do you want for them?' Steve asked. Ghost sobbed harder.

The grin seemed to throw off light, it was so wide and dazzling. 'Two apiece. Ten for all six of 'em.'

84   'Ten *dollars*?'

'Hey, I'm in a hurry, I gotta unload these puppies today, yez think this is *legal* or somethin'?'

As if on cue, sirens rose out of the general distant cacophony, approaching fast. A pair of police cars rounded the corner and came shrieking up the block. Revolving blue light flickered across the lenses of the black wrap-around shades. The grin disappeared. Without even a *good day to yez* the vendor scooped up the artificial leg and took off down the street. One car roared after him. The other slammed to a halt at the curb where Steve and Ghost still stood staring stupidly at the heads.

'You weren't really going to buy one, were you?' Ghost whispered.

''Course not.' Steve snorted. 'I don't have any money anyway, remember? The bums got it all. I'm lucky to have an ID to show this cop.' He dug out his wallet and flipped it open. 'We're just a couple of hicks from North Carolina, Officer. We lay no claim to these jars or their contents.'

Minds like butterflies preserved in brine, trapped under thick glass . . .

It seemed that their friendly vendor, a gentleman whose given name was Robyn Moorhead but who was known variously as Robyn Hood, Moorhead Robbins, and (aptly enough) 'More Head', had robbed a medical transport truck en route from Beth Israel Hospital to the Mütter 85

Medical Museum in Philadelphia while it was stopped at a gas station. The truck's door had not latched properly, and More Head and an unidentified girlfriend had simply climbed in and cleaned it out. He had already sold several items before Steve and Ghost came along. The artificial leg, though, was his own. He used it for display purposes only, to call attention to whatever shady wares he sold; it was a valuable antique and not for sale; he carried it everywhere.

No, Ghost told himself. *You did not feel their minds beating against the jars like dying insects. You did not feel the raw burn of formaldehyde against your eyeball, the dead taste of it in your mouth; you did not feel the subtle breakdown of the molecular dream that was your brain. They were not alive. You could not feel them.*

'I gotta know,' said the cop as he finished writing up their statement. 'How much did he want for 'em?' Steve told him, and the cop shrugged, then sighed. He was a decent sort and the affair seemed to have put him in a philosophical mood. 'Man, even'f I was a crook, even'f I was tryna sell yuman heads, I'd't least be askin' more'n ten bucks. Kinda devalues the sanctity a'yuman life, y'know?'

Jewelled wings, beating themselves to powder against thick glass . . .

86 They had overshot the club by five blocks. The cops

pointed them in the right direction and ten minutes later they were descending below street level again, past the unlit neon sign that said not *Beware* but *Be Aware*, though Ghost guessed it amounted to the same thing, and into the club. The poster they had sent was plastered everywhere: TONIGHT – LOST SOULS? They were too tired to consider doing a soundcheck yet, but it was just the two of them, Steve's guitar and Ghost's voice, and they didn't really need one. At any rate they wouldn't be going on till midnight. Right now they needed sleep. One of the bartenders was out of town and had left them the keys to her apartment, which was just upstairs.

Too tired for the stairs, they rode the ancient, terrifying elevator up seven stories. Steve had bummed two beers at the bar. He guzzled most of one as they rode up. 'New York is pretty interesting,' he said.

'No shit.'

Steve snorted into his beer. And then at once they were both laughing, losing it in a rickety box suspended from an antique cable in a building that was taller than any building in Missing Mile but small by the standards of this magical, morbid, million-storied city. They fell against each other and howled and slapped high-five. They were young and the one had a voice like gravelly gold and the other could play guitar with a diamond-hard edge born of sex and voodoo and despair, and it was all part of the Great Adventure.

They staggered out at the top still giggling, fumbled with three unfamiliar locks, and let themselves into the apartment. The place was decorated all in black: black walls, black lace dripping from the ceiling, black paint over the windows, black silk sheets on a huge futon that covered the floor. The effect was soothing, like being cradled in the womb of night. Their laughter wound down.

Steve stood his guitar case in a corner, gulped the second beer after Ghost refused it, and stretched his tired bones out on the futon. Ghost toed his sneakers off and lay down beside him. It was absolutely dark and, for the first time since Port Authority, nearly quiet. How strange to think that the whole teeming city was still out there, just beyond the walls of the building. Suddenly Ghost felt disoriented in the little pocket of blackness, as if the compass he always carried in his head had deserted him. He shifted on the mattress so that his shoulder touched Steve's arm, so that he could feel Steve's familiar warmth all along the left side of his body. Steve heaved a great deep sigh like a sleeping hound. Ghost thought of all the highways, all the back roads, all the train tracks and green paths that led back home, and he did not feel so far away.

And there was music, there was always music to carry him wherever he wanted to go. Soon the distant thrum of the city and the tales it wanted to tell him faded completely, and the gouge of Steve's bony elbow in his side lulled him to sleep.

PENGUIN 60s

MARTIN AMIS · *God's Dice*

HANS CHRISTIAN ANDERSEN · *The Emperor's New Clothes*

MARCUS AURELIUS · *Meditations*

JAMES BALDWIN · *Sonny's Blues*

AMBROSE BIERCE · *An Occurrence at Owl Creek Bridge*

DIRK BOGARDE · *From Le Pigeonnier*

WILLIAM BOYD · *Killing Lizards*

POPPY Z. BRITE · *His Mouth will Taste of Wormwood*

ITALO CALVINO · *Ten Italian Folktales*

ALBERT CAMUS · *Summer*

TRUMAN CAPOTE · *First and Last*

RAYMOND CHANDLER · *Goldfish*

ANTON CHEKHOV · *The Black Monk*

ROALD DAHL · *Lamb to the Slaughter*

ELIZABETH DAVID · *I'll be with You in the Squeezing of a Lemon*

N. J. DAWOOD (TRANS.) · *The Seven Voyages of Sindbad the Sailor*

ISAK DINESEN · *The Dreaming Child*

SIR ARTHUR CONAN DOYLE · *The Man with the Twisted Lip*

DICK FRANCIS · *Racing Classics*

SIGMUND FREUD · *Five Lectures on Psycho-Analysis*

KAHLIL GIBRAN · *Prophet, Madman. Wanderer*

STEPHEN JAY GOULD · *Adam's Navel*

ALASDAIR GRAY · *Five Letters from an Eastern Empire*

GRAHAM GREENE · *Under the Garden*

JAMES HERRIOT · *Seven Yorkshire Tales*

PATRICIA HIGHSMITH · *Little Tales of Misogyny*

M. R. JAMES AND R. L. STEVENSON · *The Haunted Dolls' House*

RUDYARD KIPLING · *Baa Baa, Black Sheep*

PENELOPE LIVELY · *A Long Night at Abu Simbel*

KATHERINE MANSFIELD · *The Escape*

PENGUIN 60s